Winter of
Nimue, daughter of the Queen's 'other Welsh wizard' who is herself
a 'wise child', has left London for the wilds of North Wales
in search of her destiny.

The playwright Will Shakespeare follows his enigmatic Dark Lady,
but she has already met the scarred wizard Merlin Pendragon,
lord of Pendragon tower and its powerful secrets…

Amid the snows of Yule, against a dark background of superstition,
witchcraft and land-greed for the newly-discovered Welsh gold,
the two are parted by violence, terror and fire…

DILYS GATER, a professional author for over 30 years, has written 14 novels under the pseudonym Katrina Wright which are acclaimed by a wide readership in both the UK and USA for their powerful and gripping storytelling.

A recognised authority on contemporary spirituality under her own name, she is a practising psychic and medium who has written many books on her work and now follows in the tradition of Dion Fortune, Aleister Crowley and others in presenting spiritual wisdom in fictional form.

'one of the best on both sides of the Atlantic'-
Richard Bell (Writing Magazine)

'This lady knows her subject & she knows how to write about it'
(Prediction)

The Moonlit Door Series - FICTION

Books by Dilys Gater

Non-fiction

A Psychic's Casebook
Past Lives: Case Histories
Celtic Wise Woman
The Urban Shaman
Understanding Second Sight
Understanding Spirit Guides
Understanding Star Children
Come Shining Through: Travelling Hopefully
In & Out the Windows: My Life as a Psychic
Summer with Bax: A Fresh Take on Reality
A Season with Vivien Leigh: The Life & Art of an Actress

Fiction

Pendragon: The Hand of Glory

Author's Notes

Thanks to Derek Jones of Soundings for encouraging me to write PENDRAGON and for his friendship over nearly twenty years.

It was in Herbert Hughes' Cheshire and its Welsh Border (Dennis Dobson, London 1966) that I came across the suggestion that Shakespeare might have visited Flint, which I have incorporated into this story.

PENDRAGON is a work of fiction but many of the characters factually existed, and many of the events mentioned historically happened. I have tried to keep facts and dates accurate but allowed myself a little novelist's license in places for the sake of the story.

Pendragon
The Wizard's Daughter

Dilys Gater

Anecdotes Publishing

ISBN: 9781898670 162
Text copyright © Dilys Gater 1997, 1999, 2009

This edition published by: Anecdotes
70 The Punch Bowl, Manchester Road,
Buxton, Derbyshire SK17 6TB

Printed and bound by:
Photoprint of Leek, 71 Haywood Street
Leek, Staffs ST13 5JH

For the Aetheling
The shadowy prince

Heb ddiwedd, yn dy garu du

Pendragon
The Wizard's Daughter

1

Nimue sank breathlessly onto a stone sunk deep in the earth, pushing her velvet hood back from her face. The moonlight was as bright as day, and she drank in the silvery beauty of the scene before her, a thrill clutching at her heart in spite of the melancholy situation in which she found herself, compounding confusion and grief.

She had never seen the sea, the ocean her father had spoken of so often and with such yearning, she had never imagined there could be anything so beautiful as the pale liquid fire that shimmered softly below the line of sand and the encroaching trees, throwing their deep shadows. In the heavens, the moon rode at the full, and Nimue sighed, clutching the moment to her, unwilling to share it with anyone else, especially with Gilbert.

She darted a quick glance over her shoulder at the thought of her so recently affianced betrothed. The lights of the inn sparked, bobbing with ruby brightness, on the road behind her, and she could hear voices, as Gilbert ordered the hastily roused occupants to attend to the broken wheel of the coach. Mary's high tones rose into the night sky. Nimue stopped her ears, turning impatiently back to the wonderland before her. Her breath came quickly, and her eyes, those green-golden eyes which had so often led her, unsuspecting, into difficulties with men who thought she was enticing them into dalliance, softened and widened as though she would drink in the scene.

How beautiful it was. Her father had been right, as he always had been.

'Wales is my country, even though I live in exile,' he told her often. 'And it is your country too, where your destiny lies. You are a child, a dear one, but unawakened.'

'Why don't you say what you mean?' she teased, tossing her head in its new cap of pearls, which Lord Daventry had presented only that morning, partly in deference to her beauty (as he told her ardently) but partly, she knew, to propitiate her father's power. 'I am spoiled, I am vain, I am wayward.'

He smiled, his mouth twitching with amused affection. Apart from the fact that she could housewife it with the best, so that his household lacked for nothing in cleanliness, good plain fare and the touch of a woman to soften the harsh edges of living, she was bewitching with her pert, wide-eyed face heart-shaped beneath the dark frame of her hair, outlined by the pearls. And she knew it.

'If you were not my daughter,' he began, and she interrupted, mock-seriously:

'Would you beat me?'

He laughed aloud.

'Sure someone will, child, for the havoc you create in the hearts of the likes of Lord Daventry, and that poor fool Will Shakespeare. But you forget that I can read the future. You will never find yourself here in London, only when you return to the place where you were born, where your roots lie deep, will you discover who you really are. And then you will find your true love and the desire of your heart for ever.'

Nimue remembered that laughing moment as she sat with her face turned towards the bright moonlight on the sea, and to her horror, a choked sob rose in her throat. Her dear father, gone now for ever, had been laid to rest in the English soil, to remain an exile from his native land. The earth on his grave was still newly turned, and remembrances from some of the greatest of the land who had (however secretly) known him and come to him for advice and counsel, still scented the air with fragrance. And here she was, sitting here on a rock in the far west, in a strange and mysterious land, unknown yet even though it was her birthplace, with the heavy coat-of-arms of the ancient, though slightly threadbare Stoneyathes on her betrothal finger and a man who called himself her husband-to-be, whom she hardly knew. And who, if she was honest, she was beginning to regard with some disfavour.

She was afraid it had all been a mistake, that her father, ill and wandering in his mind, had misread the chart, when he declared that Gilbert Stoneyathe was the man she was destined to marry, and hardly with the strength to do it, handed his beloved daughter into this stranger's keeping and gave his blessing to the union. He had not lingered, and by the following dawn he had been at peace – so Nimue achingly told herself as she sat for the last time beside his bed before Gilbert Stoneyathe, tight-lipped, bustled her away.

A sound roused her from her musings. A sudden cry, and a sharp ringing oath in a voice that had the urgency of a musket shot. The night had been still, apart from the sounds from the inn behind her, and the splash of the waves and the soft twitters of the night creatures in the trees that cast deep shadow some way to the right, their leaves gently soughing.

She started up, turning. Beyond the trees, at the edge of the sand where the silver foam of the waves met the polished edge of the land, there was a crashing and cursing. Nimue, staring, saw a white shape rearing as though it had risen from the sea, a white horse, she thought, dazed by the sudden apparition, a winged horse such as she had heard her father tell when he had recounted the ancient legends while the candles flickered and the winter howled round the closed shutters of their little house almost on London Bridge, the snow beat on the door and the draught whirled down the chimney into the room in flames and smoke.

7

A unicorn, perhaps, she amended her impression, for the horse did not have wings. It stood now, pawing at the waves, fetlock-deep, the water falling like drops of mercury from its hooves. It nosed, head down, at something in the water. A dark shape, like a body.

Forgetting that there was an inn behind her where lights, warmth, assistance might be obtained, Nimue ran across the sands letting her dark cloak fall and lifting her long skirt with both hands. As she approached the horse, it moved uneasily and the shape in the water stirred and began to swear even more passionately, invoking names of spirits that Nimue had heard her father use, but which sat oddly in the mouth of a stranger.

The man, clasping the mane of his horse, emerged from the waves shaking off the water and rose slowly to his feet. He seemed to Nimue to tower above her, a black figure against the moon.

'Sir, is all well?' she enquired. Her voice, for some reason unknown to herself, was shaking.

The figure abruptly stopped swearing, and there was a silence, broken only by the soft splash of the waves.

'Who the devil are you?' a harsh voice demanded.

Prompted by a strange intuition, she did not reply that she was Mistress Gwynne, betrothed to Gilbert Stoneyathe, newly of Grannah, and that it would behove this rough fellow to keep a civil tongue in his head. Instead, she found herself saying in a breathless half-whisper:

'My name is Nimue.'

There was another silence, then unexpectedly he laughed, but there was something strange and wild and hard about his laughter.

'Is it indeed? And what if I told you mine was Merlin?'

Nimue drew her breath in sharply. It seemed suddenly as though she stood in a dream, in the silver moonlight, this dark shadow looming before her, the white horse standing quietly now, his hand on its neck.

'I have heard the story of Merlin and Nimue,' she said after a moment. 'My father told me the tales of King Arthur. Merlin was the magician, and Nimue was his love who trapped him with his own magic and kept him a prisoner.'

'Then it seems I must beware of you, lest you do me harm,' the cold voice said. 'Do not enter my domain, and do not trespass within my boundaries. Women are the very devil, and your eyes I see are larger than most, more potent for ill-wishing. You are obviously some fiend in human form, sent by the evil one to tempt me in my moment of weakness.'

Nimue began to bristle. She was not accustomed to such words from masculine lips.

'If I had intended to tempt you, sir, I would have chosen my moment far more carefully,' she told him. 'And I would have made certain that I succeeded.'

And with that parting shot, she turned on her heel and walked, in quivering fury, towards the trees and the lights of the inn beyond. Behind her, she thought she heard a quick, smothered guffaw of appreciation. But when she haughtily turned her head, the white horse and its rider were some distance away, weaving into the moonlight as though they had not been real.

Thoughtfully she retrieved her cloak and began to walk back to the inn, the magic of the night gone. Perhaps, indeed, they had not been real. Yet somehow that cold, hard voice seemed to echo much more clearly in her brain than the light, civilised tones of her betrothed as he came forward frowning in the torchlight.

'Nimue, what mischief have you been making? We cannot proceed until morning, confound it, and Mary is fainting with exhaustion. We will lodge here for the rest of the night, so oblige me by going to your chamber and consoling my sister in a proper manner rather than disappearing into the dark like a wanton. If our union is to be strong, I must be able to rely on you.'

Stung, Nimue lifted her head coldly.

'Am I then to be nursemaid to your sister for the rest of my life, Gilbert? That was not what you promised my father when he agreed to let you marry me.'

'Do not open discussions at this hour, any grievances you have can be aired tomorrow, in a more suitably discreet manner in a private room,' he said brusquely. 'I realise you are tired, but so am I, so is Mary and the coachman, and so may I add are the horses, for whom I parted with an inordinately large amount of money. Do not force me to have to make allowances for your lack of breeding.'

The words seemed to hang between them, burning like words of fire into the night and into Nimue's mind and heart. There was a short silence. Even Gilbert seemed appalled at what he had said. He made a quick gesture, and took a step towards her, but she drew herself into her cloak with a movement that, though hardly more than a slight shrug, stopped him in his tracks. Then she spoke in even tones.

'Very well Gilbert. I am sorry you have been inconvenienced. If one of the people will light me to my chamber, I will go to Mary.'

'Nimue - ,' he began, still finding it difficult to speak her name directly, but she turned.

'I understand perfectly. There is no need to say more. You will not have me trying your patience again with my lack of breeding.'

'I did not mean - ,' he began uneasily, but her dark cloak had melted into the shadows of the doorway behind her and she had gone.

Mary Stoneyathe, dainty as a delicate flower in her pale blue satin, creased now and travel-stained, seemed wilted in the extreme and was sitting in the best chamber the inn could offer, fanning herself with her cambric kerchief. Her pale face was drawn and ashen with fatigue, her silver-gilt hair wisping from her blue velvet cap. On the tray before her a hastily assembled meal of meat and bread, with a goblet of wine, was untasted.

'Oh, I think I shall die,' she moaned, as Nimue entered the chamber. 'This country is barbarous, and I am certain that every one of my bones is in pieces from the jolting of the coach and that broken wheel.'

'Take what rest you can, then,' Nimue advised, eyeing the more than adequate tester bed that brooded against the darkly panelled inner wall of the chamber. 'I fully intend to. And I presume the refreshments were intended for both of us.'

Without further ado she hung up her cloak, seated herself on an oak chest at the foot of the bed and picked up a leg of chicken which she began to nibble hungrily. It seemed a long time since they had stopped on this stage of their journey from Chester.

Mary began to wail. 'Have you no sympathy for my distress, my absolute agony? Oh, it is all very well for you - .'

'And precisely what does that mean?' Nimue asked dangerously.

Mary, provoked, began to cry, crystal tears shining in her wide blue eyes, and she wiped them from her thick silvery lashes.

'I cannot think why Gilbert wanted to marry you,' she hissed, though to Nimue's unwilling amusement, the words sounded more like the petulant spitting of a pretty kitten than a ringing indictment of her own shortcomings from the lips of a fine lady. 'You have no feelings, no sensitivity. And no sense of gratitude whatsoever. After all, if it were not for Gilbert - .'

'If it were not for Gilbert, I might have been sleeping in Lord Daventry's bed, safely wedded and newly Her Ladyship,' Nimue shrugged, with a fine disregard for probability but attempting to be flippant, for Mary's words cut dangerously near to the painful truth of her situation. 'He asked me enough times. And Will Shakespeare, the actor, offered me some very interesting propositions too, which made up in passion for what they lacked in terms of a wedding ring. Poor man, he could not sleep for writing sonnets to my eyes.'

Mary had stopped crying and was watching Nimue in wonder.

'You know your father left you with nothing. And such a reputation. Are you really a witch, as people say?'

Thoughtfully Nimue placed the chicken bone down, dipped her slim white fingers in the rosewater that had been provided and lifted the goblet of wine. This, she was telling herself, was what she must expect in the future from the ignorant, the credulous. It did no good to burn with fury, to feel she must defend her father's good name and her own. The gossips would never understand, and the sooner she learned the better not to let such barbed arrows find a mark but to glance off without hurt. She was beginning to realise that far from being proud of being her father's daughter, she must learn to be discreet. It could be dangerous to talk of such things, and there was no-one now to protect her.

'My father was an astrologer,' she said mildly. 'Like Doctor Dee, who has advised the Queen openly.'

'They say Eliza came to your father also, but for dark dealings,' Mary told her and Nimue was hard put to control her outrage and disgust at the young woman's insinuating words. She was studying her brother's intended bride as though Nimue was a freak at a fair. 'The other Welsh wizard, that is what they called him at Court. Can you work spells and magic?' Unexpectedly she lowered her voice. 'Can you get me a husband?'

Nimue choked down the incredulous laughter, the hot distasteful words that sprang to her lips, the desire to rush from the room, from the inn. She forced herself instead to sit calmly, lowering her fine dark lashes so that Mary should not see her eyes.

'Perhaps.'

For it would be as well, she realised with a chill of ice settling between her shoulder blades, to hide the true facts, to imply that she was indeed familiar with the powers of darkness. Alone in the world, her fate now in the hands of Gilbert Stoneyathe and his feather-pated sister, she might need their dubious assistance.

Mary was silent, and Nimue rose and stretched.

'I am tired,' she said. 'I need to sleep, even if you choose to sit up and brood on your wrongs.'

But it appeared that Mary's mind was running in different directions than her wrongs, her attention diverted by the prospect of deep and sinister doings.

'You have certainly come to the right place, at any rate,' she said waspishly. 'There is another wizard here, I remember my cousin David speaking of him years ago, when he braved the roads to come to London for the Yule festivities. He can pull lightning bolts from the sky and make curses. He lives in a turret on the top of a hill with the devil, and wolves and demons taught him the Black Arts.'

Into Nimue's mind, with no prompting at all, came a picture of the dark figure which had towered over her at the waves' edge, his hand on the neck of his white horse. And into her ears floated the recollection of the words he had used when he had supposed himself alone.

'Merlin,' she murmured. 'The enchanter. I think I have seen him, tall as a forest tree with a voice like thunder, riding a horse that comes from the sea.'

Mary, pettishly bending to remove her velvet shoes, which were far too elaborate for travelling, remarked:

'Merlin Pendragon, yes, that was his name, but I doubt his voice is like thunder. He was an old man when my cousin David spoke of him, he must be an ancient by now. Bent too, like a gnarled old tree with the rheums in his bones, I heard David tell, and frightened me so that I hid in the press, because I thought the wizard would take me off after I stole a

13

sweetmeat and boil me in his great black cauldron and gnaw on my bones.'

Nimue was feeling very weary. She lay in her underskirt, unable to rest, while the end of the candle flickered itself out and Mary, beside her, moved and moaned, begrudging that they must share the tester.

'When we get to the House, I will make sure that the best room is mine. And the best bed. I have not suffered travelling all this way for nothing and burying myself in this dreadful country,' she fretted. 'If I did not feel too utterly exhausted I would insist that Gilbert turned the coach round and returned to London.'

Nimue hardly heard her words. She was thinking of the way the candle had flickered and leaped a week ago as she watched beside her father's bed, soothing his hot forehead with a cloth moistened with herbs in vinegar. It portended a death, Arabella Nevile had said, when she called briefly to bring gifts from the Court, tall and dark in her sweeping habit, the groom holding her restless horse at the door.

'You know it must come, Nimue. You should take care for yourself, there are many who have no love for your father.'

Nimue, clutching the packages which she knew had come directly from the most royal hand in the kingdom, one who esteemed her father's counsel well, was exhausted with watching and her eyes gritty with unshed tears.

'But, the Queen - .'

Arabella's voice was dark.

'Foolish child. Her Grace can do nothing for you. She above all knows that power begets enemies, and while she sends to her other Welsh wizard in secret while he is alive she will not lift a finger for his daughter when he is dead. You must look to yourself.'

And, Nimue thought as the candle still flickered and her eyes burned at the recollection, how it had seemed like fate, like destiny, when Gilbert Stoneyathe, closeted with her father in his sickroom, had emerged to tell her that permission had been given for him to take her to his newly-inherited estates in Wales as his bride.

Her father's voice, thin and breathless.

'The charts, Nimue – in the west, it must be Stoneyathe – go with him, take my blessing – no dowry but my love - .'

She stirred, wanting to forget those heavy hours before the dawn. Deep in shock and grief, she had carried out her father's wishes, and pledged herself to Stoneyathe, left her home with him when her father was decently buried, for his Welsh estates. But now, as she lay beside the sleeping Mary, she could feel that the many differences between them on the journey, coldnesses and isolation, had been like straws in the wind, pointers in another direction. And foreboding gathered in her heart.

2

She had seen the great black Donjon of the castle of Flint, circled with crying seabirds, looming in the mist of an autumn morning. And inland, the hazy red sun hanging low over hills where the thorns of winter were already gathering beneath the still lush berries of early October. With her inner eye, Nimue had visualised the fast, dark waters that would run beneath the heavy, snow-laden crusts of ice, the stillness of the trees as the year turned, and she had felt an involuntary lifting of her heart.

At the shrine of Saint Winefride, Gilbert had ostentatiously broken their journey to give thanks for his inheritance, though his nature was too unemotional for him to be a sincerely religious man. He felt, however, that some sort of gesture was needed in the eyes of the world, for his grant of the manor of Grannah had indeed been a gift from heaven, saving both him and his sister from their drab, penny-pinching existence eking

15

out years as dependants, hangers-on at the Court, clutching at the glories of the Stoneyathes' past.

And it was at the shrine that Nimue had felt it most strongly, the spell of this land of her birth. Within the shadowed vaults, gilded by the luminous glow of the candles lit by those pilgrims who had come to the Saint, praying for a miracle, incense lay thick as smoke on the air, and the voices of monks and sisters, dispersed long since when King Hal had turned them out to starve and thrown down the walls of their abbeys and nunneries, seemed to be still rich and sweet in her ears. The surface of the holy well puckered in glints of delicate brightness, and Nimue, one more pilgrim petitioning the virgin Winefride, had made her own prayer to the Saint while her fingers lightly touched her forehead and throat, wet with water from the sacred spring.

'You died a death rather than give yourself to a man, but I can feel my soul quicken in this land where my father has foreseen my destiny. Is Gilbert my rightful fate? Is he my true mate, the one who will warm my heart and my bed, or were my father's eyes blinded with the glory of his passing and visions of the place where he longed to be, and my mother's lips welcoming him home?'

She waited for some answer but there was only the gentle wavering of the holy spring, and Mary's petulant voice beside her.

'Oh, do let us get on. I am perishing of thirst, Gilbert. How much longer will this dreadful journey take?'

And when at last she stepped down before the great door of Grannah, and saw the sweeping sky race above the dark bulk of the hills that enclosed the soft hollow where Gilbert Stoneyathe's long distant ancestor had built, only half taming the wild wooded countryside and creating tangled plots of gardens that were roughly tended now, with the red berries of the rowans splashed like the blood of old battles against the encroaching trees, Nimue felt as though she had passed through a strange, mystical metamorphosis.

Where was the girl who, with dark rags of unexpressed grief gathered tightly about her, had turned her back on London and the past? Gilbert and his sister appeared to have become even more entrenched in their painfully alien personalities as they had journeyed into this Celtic land but she was aware of visions, visitations, expanding of the horizons, and the edge of her loss had been dulled by the dawning of a new maturity, subtly communicated from this country of her forebears. Whatever was to befall her, she was glad, after all, that she had come.

The Welsh servants and men of the household, roughly garbed and dark-browed, smelling of the land, attended on their arrival, and there were curious but almost furtive glances, and the quick cut and thrust of words in the Welsh tongue. Food and drink was hastily prepared and brought into the parlour, where the travellers were gathered in a forlorn group, huddled into their cloaks against the chill. There was no fire, since they were not awaited, and Mary shivered, unable to eat, and hardly warmed when a fire was newly lighted and began to burn bravely. She was worn and weary, in a sorry state, and at Gilbert's request, diffidently made, Nimue went with her after they had eaten to attend to her wants. She felt as though she was caring for a fractious child.

It was some time later, and the day drawing in when at last she had seen to the household affairs occasioned by their arrival and was free to go to the chamber that now awaited her ready prepared for slumber, and she entered it gratefully in the wake of the plump, heavy-featured woman in the dark dress who was called Morfydd, and who had had the charge of the house, there being no mistress.

Dismissing the woman, Nimue was glad to be alone, and in the light of the candle that Morfydd had set down, she looked around her. The chamber was tidy, though cursorily swept and

17

with the webs of little spiders daintily festooning the dark panelling and carving on the bedposts. She would have it aired and cleaned tomorrow. But tonight it smelled of damp, and she crumpled her skirts on the window seat and pushed the casement open so that draughts of sweet air with a faint far-off tang of the tops of mountains and still pools haunted by spirits of the air and water, came surging through. The evening was well advanced, and there was a softness to the dark that seemed to touch her almost physically. It seemed to her like the welcome of an old friend, and she paused, savouring it. Then she turned to the satchels that had been brought in from the coach and placed at the foot of the bed with its heavy coverlet and fur comforter.

Gilbert had bade her a formal good night, and gone to attend to such further matters that needed his attention, and in the adjoining chamber, Mary was deep in an exhausted slumber with the coverlet pulled high round her ears, and her pale hair tumbled round her delicate face. Her bed was cosy from the warming pan Nimue had filled herself with coals from the fire in the cavernous kitchen, and her right foot, which she had twisted in her velvet shoes at the shrine of the Saint, and which had made her sick and faint from the pain for the rest of the journey, was propped up on a huge mound of cushions.

Regarding her dispassionately as she slept, Nimue had decided that there would probably be no difficulty in finding the required husband for this exotic little bird, a man would lust to hold her tiny body in his hands like a jewelled plaything, and then, unnerved by her fragility, would not dare to touch. But in the strangeness of the ways of attraction between lovers, Mary Stoneyathe was her own worst enemy. She might have had anyone she chose, even at the Court, and as for the country lads and hulking Celtic savages they had encountered on their journey, they had gawped, dazzled, as though she were a creature of wonder from a distant star. But an hour in Mary's company drove away those she most yearned for, and the cloddish admiration of lesser beings had her petulantly biting her lips and pouting, giving way to the ever-ready tears of frustration.

Nimue had more important things to do than to dwell on her future sister's marital prospects, however. She wanted to consider her own, and before matters passed from her control entirely. It was true that she and Gilbert were formally betrothed, and that she had promised her father she would marry him. It was true that if she did not, she might find herself homeless in this strange land, in the same state as those poor monks and sisters had been when King Harry had barred the monastery and nunnery doors to them and they had trudged, sick at heart, to beg their bread, only their rosary beads to comfort them against the cold of charity. But if her father had been mistaken, if Gilbert Stoneyathe was not the true lord of her heart – and Nimue was becoming increasingly sure that he was not – if he was not, what then?

She had brought only two rough leathern satchels with her from London, the baggage was following them on a lumbering cart. Within the satchels, however, were all that she prized, her father's books and charts and the strange and secret objects of his calling that Nimue had grown up with. The heavy crystal that glowed with mysterious depths, holding the light in splinters, in fragments, in rainbows and in a still shining like a gathered drop of pale ice. It was cool in the twilight as she unwrapped the silken cloth and laid it before her on the wooden floor, and its coolness calmed her heart. The crystal would tell her the truth.

'Hold to the light,' her father had taught her, at all the times when she coaxed him, with childlike inquisitiveness, to reveal the secrets of his calling and she had laughed.

'What of the spirits to be summoned at my will, Father, so that I may possess all I desire?'

Gereint Gwynne's dark eyes had been luminous with knowledge as they rested on the eager young face.

'When the time comes for you to summon spirits, you will know of it. But until then, it is enough to hold to the light.'

And as the years had passed, she came to understand that the summoning of spirits to obtain all desires mattered little, measured against the awareness of the light that had been with her since her birth. Her father taught her the rudiments of the study of the heavens, the stars and planets, the skills of mathematics, so that she was as familiar with natal charts as he, but her heart was not in it, and he told her that was because she had been born a wise child, one who could see with other eyes, rather than pore over the meridians and the midheavens with quill and parchment, compasses and instruments.

When she complained that she could see nothing with other eyes, he said, smiling: 'You do not know what you see. When the time comes for you to know, you will know of it.'

But she had learned that the visions come unannounced, as familiar as the touch of the sun and the wind and the rain, so that they are not visions at all, but knowledge that was always known.

Her father had given her his great crystal two days before he died. That and the books, filled with calculations and words that held the powers in check.

'John Dee is seeking the philosophers' stone,' he told her, his breath rasping in his fevered chest. 'All of them would turn base metal to gold. But there are many kinds of alchemy, Nimue. Never forget that love is the greatest alchemist of all.'

And now, she bent over the crystal, young and untried against the ways of the dark, her eyes focussed on the shifting depths of light as she sought to see what the future held for her in this land, in this house. In the depths of her grief, she had not thought to wonder exactly why Gilbert Stoneyathe had asked to marry her, it had been enough that he had asked and her father had wished it, but now she sought for answers in the crystal.

He had not known her, but he had seen her, laughing, dancing, simply enough on the Green at Michaelmas, and he had been swept by a glance from her eyes, golden-green, though she had been unaware. And because of this, he had come to her father, unannounced, not knowing of Gereint Gwynne's fatal illness, to ask if he might have Nimue.

But he had never mentioned love, she realised now. He had been bewitched by her eyes like Will Shakespeare, like Lord Daventry, like all of them. Enthralled. No longer master of himself. And he was leaving London for the wilds of Wales to take up his inheritance. Of course, it had been too sudden, like summer lightning, brief and then gone. It had been ill-starred, ill advised. He did not love her. He did not know her. And she did not love him.

But because of the word of a dying man, her father straining his fading eyes over the charts, wanting to believe this was the true destiny for the daughter he must leave alone and unprotected, their fates were linked. The days they had spent on the road with Mary passed through her mind like the scenes of a mummers' play. Though her image might have ridden with him, and haunted his bed, keeping him from sleep, the woman herself he had found difficult, ill-bred, strange. He had kissed her only once, stiffly, to seal the betrothal pledge, and kept from her in the days that followed, watching her. The fascination of her eyes had melted before his impatience for a docile, compliant mate, one who recognised her superior and knew her place. Gilbert Stoneyathe was descended from the princely lords of Wales, however thinly and indirectly their blood ran in him, however alienated over the years at the English Court and the struggle to survive in the face of poverty. His wife must be aware of this fact and respect it.

But Nimue, the off-spring of a dubious passion between a Welsh wizard and the anonymous wayward daughter (some said) of a great house who had died giving birth, was a bastard. She might have been expected to be duly grateful for the

21

honour Gilbert was bestowing upon her, but she did not even seem aware that there was anything at all lacking in her own blood line. And the fascination of her eyes, which had seemed to promise so much, withdrew from him, flickering as dangerously as the marsh-lights, the will o' the wisp that drew mortal men into places where the earth was uneasy beneath their feet, and they might be lost.

Gilbert Stoneyathe, too late, had realised he was treading on ground which was not for him, and each evening since her father had handed her into his keeping, he had knelt in uneasy prayer and crossed himself, asking for deliverance, but whether from himself or from his betrothed bride, or from some darker fate, he did not know.

Nimue saw in the crystal that Gilbert Stoneyathe was a man torn between seething, though unexpressed passions, and feeling her helplessness, she buried her face in her clasped hands. Was her destiny to be decided by the uneasy conscience of weakness? Where was the great flame her father had seen burning in the west?

She knelt again, looking deep into the heart of the crystal. There *was* a flame – a flame – flames that devoured, flames that destroyed as well as gave out warmth - . Within her inner eye she saw fire burning, flames leaping fifty feet into the air, sparks bursting in handfuls as though flung by some devilish glee against the face of the night. Her inner ear heard the boom of exploding timbers, crashing into the heart of the conflagration, and over all, even as her spirit sank within her breast at the horror of it, her skin feeling the searing heat in the moments before it blistered and blackened into charred flakes of ash, she heard a voice, rushing on the night wind.

'My love, my love, my love,' it mourned.

Was it her own voice, which lifted the hairs upon her head with a coldness so intense that she knew it for the touch of a dead hand? Or was it the voice of another? Overcome, still in the grip of the vision, she reached for the little cross made from iron horseshoe nails that hung always between her breasts on a twisted thread of silk.

Fire. If this was to be her fate, she could not stop it, her father had taught her that. Her life was already written in the book of the Recording Angel, her fate decided. For long moments, her heart failing within her, she shrank from what the future might hold. But Gereint Gwynne had also instructed his daughter to look, clear-eyed, at fear and confront it. So, on the uneven boards of the little chamber which marked the end of her journey – or perhaps, she thought uncertainly, the true beginning – she bent her head with the soft fluff of dark curls childishly tousled in disarray, and consciously submitted her will to the power that guarded the flight of the sparrow, and the fall of the leaf, laying her destiny in its keeping. She prayed only for the courage to face whatever was to come. Then, suddenly exhausted and with the roaring of the flames, dream-like, still hollow in her ears, she wrapped the crystal carefully in its silken cloth and replaced it in the leathern satchel. Then, taking no care for her heavy long skirt and velvet bodice, she lay down upon the patchwork on the bed, pulling the fur comforter close around her, blowing out her candle. In the darkness, filled with night sounds she could not identify, she slept.

The morning brought rain, in silver rods against the casement, but Nimue was not aware of it until a clattering of hooves, barking of dogs and squawking of querulous hens and a voice bellowing below her window roused her. Heavy-headed, and stiff in her crumpled gown, she sat up.

'Dorabella! Dorabella! Damn your eyes, girl, come out, come out I say!' someone cried in a deep baritone, and as the hens continued to squawk and the dogs to bark and the men in the yard to call back in the strange foreign tongue that was the language of this wild country – sounding something like the liquid rushing of the waters that they had heard everywhere as they made their way along the treacherous tracks to Grannah,

Nimue thought – she went to the window to see a man on a great horse holding his beast in check even as he set it prancing with his roars. The dogs were leaping about him, and the servants scurrying in the rain like ants, here and there. There were rivers through the yard, and the sky was heavy. She was aware of hills crouched, even mountains at no great distance even though she could not see them through the mist.

Then she heard Gilbert's voice below at the great doorway, cool, haughty, demanding to know the stranger's business. The man stopped in mid-bellow, and stared, then swept off a hat from which the plumes draggled, soaking.

'The devil! Is it the heir?, sir, you have arrived? A thousand pardons, I would not have disturbed you for the world, but for my daughter, Dorabella, who like the eternal minx she is, has run off in a pet.'

'But why should you assume I have the child here?' Gilbert enquired. Nimue was aware, even on her short acquaintance with him, that he was holding his irritation in check with difficulty.

The stranger removed his bulk from his horse, and tossed the reins to a nearby lad, advancing on Gilbert with gauntleted hand.

'It will be a new regime now, I can see that,' he grinned. 'No more laxity, no more of Dorabella sitting at the harp and singing in the twilight, or whatever else nonsense she has thought fit to indulge in. A new broom – well, long overdue, long overdue. Your cousin was a fine man, but an upholder of irregular living, no sense of his position, no sense of responsibility, God rest his soul. I knew him well, these forty years, in good times and bad. Jonas Mowas is my name, at your service sir, Mowas of Caercerrig.'

Leaning forward, Nimue saw Gilbert, obviously appeased, grasp the proffered hand.

'Will you come in, sir? We arrived only last night – and as for your daughter, I know nothing of her. Only my sister and - .'

He hesitated, and then went on in a distinctly clipped tone: ' – only my sister and Mistress Gwynne are in the house.'

As the two of them disappeared from her view, Nimue continued to sit where she was, her bones suddenly chilled. Gilbert had been about to say that his sister and his affianced wife were with him but prudence – or cowardice, she thought with sudden heat flaring in her cheeks – had checked his tongue. What tortuous thoughts were passing through his mind? She must know. Hastily splashing her face with water from the basin, and straightening her gown, looking round for a mirror and, seeing none, twisting her fingers through her hair to lift her curls into shape, she went from the room.

'Whether you go to meet God or the devil, Nimue,' her father had told her, and she recalled his words now as she paused at the top of the narrow stairs in the shadows dimmed by the rainy morning, taking deep breaths to steady herself. 'Whether you go to meet God or the devil, hold up your head and look him in the eyes.'

With straight back and lifted chin – for even if Gilbert intended to disown her, she would never let him or anyone else see that Gereint Gwynne's daughter could be afraid – she began to descend the stairs.

Dorabella Mowas, it appeared, was no child, she was a woman grown, and headstrong and wilful, though you would not have thought so, Jonas Mowas informed Gilbert ruefully, since she was but a slip of a thing, and cast her eyes down and said 'Yes' and 'No', and then did exactly as she pleased. It did not help matters, he went on, that she had been shamefully indulged, even encouraged to defy her father by Gilbert's cousin David, who unfortunately was a man of marked eccentricity that was tolerated by the local gentry only because of his breeding. His attitude towards servants, animals and women bespoke a complete lack of any sense of proper firmness whatsoever.

Now well away on the tide of his rhetoric, Jonas Mowas became oratorical. Had they considered themselves arbiters of society, Gilbert's cousin David and the old wizard, Merlin Pendragon? Cutting through the admonitions of fathers and those who knew what was best for everyone? Jonas was a Justice, no less, but had they considered that? Oh, a fine pair they had made between them, (he broke off momentarily to accept a cup of ale and to take further breath), the wizard damning honest souls to perdition with his spells and frightening the maids, not to mention the hens and cattle, so that the eggs addled and the cheese curdled and the butter would not set. Cousin David had, begging Gilbert's pardon, been no better, forever going out of his way to make trouble for those who did not share his views.

Jonas Mowas needed little encouragement to elaborate on his theme, and at Gilbert's polite show of interest (for he had hardly known his distant cousin), the sad truth was further revealed. At public festivals, whenever the wizard had appeared, a gaunt figure in his long dark cloak and hat of tawny fox complete with the tail of the beast hanging down his back, he had terrified all with his very presence, though Jonas admitted rather grudgingly that Pendragon had never actually done anything to disturb the peace – indeed, he had never made any claims to be a wizard at all, declaring merely that he chose to follow the 'old religion', but that was by the way. It was obvious that he was hand in glove with demons.

Gilbert's cousin David, on the other hand, had brought the wrath of the reluctant judiciary upon himself and cracked pates and bruised shins on those who tried to restrain him, many times because of his unfortunate habit of letting loose bears that had promised fine sport, interfering at cockfights, even those of mere beardless boys who had been reduced to unmanly tears when their birds were unceremoniously scattered and the sport turned into a rout.

Jonas shook a doleful head as he recounted how on some disastrous occasions, cousin David had aided the escape of hare or doe, beating off hounds and hunters alike with his long staff. It had even been rumoured – though this Jonas could not believe, he said weightily – that the misguided man had been heard to declare that he did not approve of war, which, begging Gilbert's pardon again, was a clear indication that he was as near mad as a gentleman might ever get.

Dorabella Mowas, however, had thought differently to her parent, and declared that cousin David was a saint. She, apparently, had been in the habit of spending long hours at Grannah instead of being about her duties, and because her father, a widower long since, found it impossible to administer the necessary beatings which might have curbed her spirit, she had remained unpunished.

'Wanton behaviour, for all that there was no real harm in it,' Jonas Mowas explained to Gilbert over his cup of ale. The parlour was swept and the fire burning brightly this morning, although the rain streamed on the last of the roses outside the casement so that the chamber seemed to swim in a watery haze. 'Your cousin was the soul of honour, I would have trusted him with Dorabella with my life, but it looks bad, Stoneyathe, yes, it looks bad when a man has no control over his own child. David used to say he loved her like the girl he lost, and after his own Gwenllian died I had not the heart to forbid Dorabella his house. She got to running off at the slightest provocation, even tears, if you like, at the cruelty of her Dada when he came to fetch her home. Cruelty, mind you! And tears!'

He fingered his beard gingerly, looking hunted.

'And you thought she might have come here this morning?' Gilbert enquired, letting the sentence hang delicately.

'She loved this house,' Jonas said simply. 'I would rather live at Grannah than old Caercerrig any day, Dada, she told me, to spite me. Knows what she will not have, too, mind. She might have been married twice before she was sixteen, good solid gentlemen who would have let her have her way, though they would have lived to regret it in my opinion, knowing Dorabella as I do, but she would not have them.'

Hearing a movement at the doorway he turned, breaking off in mid-flow. When he saw Nimue's slight figure, upright in her dark velvet, he was on his feet in a moment, despite his bulk, making her a deep reverence. 'Mistress Stoneyathe, your servant ma'am.'

There was a silence which seemed to stretch out like a pulled thread of silk, thin and tight on the air, then Gilbert said deliberately: 'It is not my sister, this is Mistress Gwynne, my sister's pensioner.'

Jonas Mowas was the least sensitive of men, but even he could not help but be aware from Nimue's cool silence and Gilbert's direct stare into her gold-green eyes as though he defied her to challenge what he had said, that there was something very wrong between them. After a few moments more of stilted enquiries as to their journey and how she liked his country – Nimue politely replying with composure that it was her country too, since she had been born in Wales – he took his leave, sending his best to Mistress Mary, and blundered out into the rain, scattering dogs, hens and servants in his progress from the house. Gilbert and Nimue remained, still staring at each other.

She said nothing, and after a moment, he turned away awkwardly.

'I – thought it best.'

'Your sister's pensioner?' Nimue's voice was low and shaking. He could not see, but her hands were clenched tightly, pressed against the skirt of her gown, very white against the dark velvet. 'For that at least, thanks. You do not intend for me to be a servant, then? I am not to maid it for Mary?'

Gilbert's face reddened. He would not meet her eyes, though the force of his discomfiture had brought an unaccustomed passion to his features. Nimue learned in that moment how unintended entanglement in love can make a man turn, at bay, to a creature that will destroy the object of his former worship in shame for seeming weakness. And her heart was suddenly quite cold, as though it had turned to ice in her breast.

'I will not break my word to your father,' he said uncomfortably. 'I will provide for you.' He made a gesture. 'Mary will want a companion, it will not be easy for her here. But for the rest - .'

His mouth thinned suddenly, and Nimue found herself regarding him almost with pity, though she was only too conscious that her future in the house depended on his goodwill, which might easily be swayed by his whim or mood of the moment.

'I have no choice in the matter, it seems,' she said slowly. 'But I cannot but think, Gilbert, that in spite of the wrong you have done me, it is what my father would have wished if he could have lived. You are no fit husband for me and I no wife for you.'

She took the heavy ring with the coat of arms from her finger and held it out to him. The light from the casement gleamed dully upon it, turning the gold to rain-washed pewter.

'I release you from the promises you made to my father and to me. And because I must eat, I will be Mary's pensioner and bear her company until time and the fates shall decree otherwise.'

3

The rain continued to fall steadily, so that the days were awash and the nights moonless black and starless. Their journey to the north had brought them from gracious late summer into tempestuous autumn, and Mary shivered in her satins and laces as she sat fretting, a piece of untidy embroidery work in her hands, her foot ostentatiously propped up beside the fire. Although her foot now appeared to be completely healed, she declared herself quite unable even to hobble.

Though, as she told Gilbert waspishly, there was little enough for her to hobble *for*. She could see nothing through the mist and torrents of this terrible place, they might be lost in the middle of those vast wastes of ocean which Drake and Frobisher and that tease Walter Raleigh spoke of, with not another vessel on the horizon. Mary bravely choked down her misery and frustration but declared yet again that she had been better to have stayed in London, even trying to make ends meet on their tiny pension and straightened beyond endurance at their threadbare lodging. At least there had been music, dancing and the admiration of men —for all that they had not been the men she wanted – to divert her.

'And here it is no better, for all that it is a manor with land, Gilbert. What land? You must turn into a labourer of your own soil, a shepherd and stinking of the midden. And there is no more money, and not even a pedlar passing for me to buy ribbons. Rocks and rivers and forest, no road, nothing. And not a civilised soul for miles, only these savages who cannot even speak the Queen's English. Indeed, indeed I do not believe I shall survive.'

Gilbert, whose abstracted attention was on matters of the estate, which had been occupying him in earnest since arrival at Grannah, regarded her with a slight impatient frown. There was colour in her cheeks from the fire that brightened the dark panelling of the parlour, and she looked very dainty and very helpless with her wide skirts pulled up to reveal her foot in its velvet slipper resting on a stool. But she had the appearance of a Bird of Paradise that has landed in a chicken coop and finds that it is itself and not the hens which is out of countenance.

'This is not the Court, I know, but there will be invitations. We are newcomers. Give them time,' he said rather wearily, and could not help adding in a tone that was dry, despite himself: 'Nimue seems to manage to be happy enough.'

Mary sprang, all kitten-claws, upon his words, retorting shrilly: 'And is that any wonder? She does as she likes, no sense at all of the true aristocrat's responsibility to duty. I thought she was to be my pensioner, that she was to earn her bread by attending to me, but she is never here and I must pine for company. What do you let her do all day to amuse herself?'

Gilbert, a man who had been discovering many things about himself within the past weeks, much to his discomfiture, would have liked to agree with her, but honesty forced him to admit the truth.

'She does not amuse herself, Mary. She has been helping me with the estate papers and business, and housewifing it, putting the house in order. And did she not ease your foot with her remedies?'

'She put arnica round the swelling and it soothed the bruises,' his sister admitted grudgingly, adding: 'And she has said she will get me a husband.'

Gilbert was stung into curious speech.

'And how will she do that, pray?'

Mary considered. She had no idea how Nimue proposed to find her that difficult commodity, a bridegroom.

'She is gathering herbs and will prepare a brew when the moon is right, and when I drink I will see the face of my lover,' she declared complacently after a moment. 'Or something of the sort, I have no doubt. I heard Mary Radcliffe tell of a witch who conjured up a lover for her by such means. And Nimue can at least make a fine posset too, and I am thirsty. Where is she, Gilbert?'

'I have sent her with a letter to Flint, to our cousin David's man of law,' Gilbert said shortly. 'It is private business. I do not understand the gabbling of these people – but I can at least trust her.'

Mary regarded him quizzically.

31

'I cannot understand you, Gilbert. First you were fiery for her and then you would not have her and you do not seem to know your mind even now. She turns you round her finger. Oh, say what you like, but it is obvious to me that you are still her slave though you try to pretend otherwise. I suppose,' she added thoughtfully, 'that she has cast a spell to keep you ensnared.'

'A spell?' he repeated, stung by her words because he knew that in some sense they were true.

Mary leaned back in her chair, a gleam in her eyes.

'Tied a thread around a moppet of wax, with a lock of your hair upon it and perhaps a fingernail, if she could get one. There must be ways and means. Well, I hope her spells to find me a husband work just as powerfully. I have never seen you in such a distraction before.'

Gilbert did not answer. In a stiff-lipped silence, he left her staring hungrily into the bright flames of the fire.

Nimue, unaware, was resting her pony beneath the dripping branches of a great oak, where tatters of mist hang tangled. There was a rocky outcrop, black rock silvered with the rain, and beyond, spread before her, the green land lay tossed and outspread like a quilt, pierced with black and darker green where the forest was thick, with the dark shapes of birds sharp above it.

She felt herself free as one of those birds, soaring on the wind, into the rain, and she turned to the boy beside her, laughing, and said impulsively, using one of the words of his language that she had learned:

'It is like another world, Llew *bach*, just created.'

The thin face laughed back, though it was doubtful whether Llew had understood her. But that did not matter, Nimue felt as though there were other tongues, other means of communication here, the very air hummed with knowledge and wisdom and power. The boy touched the flanks of his pony with his heels, and Nimue followed suit, and they started down to the world below, where the dull steely gleam of the great wide estuary of the Dee mingled with the mist, and the far banks rose muted and crouching mysteriously as the hills of a kingdom of dreams that could not be real. The morning had been exhilarating, her errand an adventure, and she was prepared to live the moment to the full in a glorious sensation of release away from the ever-demanding cares of the household at Grannah. The noon sun was attempting to break in red shafts of light through the clouds, massy in the wide sky, when she saw the towers of Flint Castle and the clustered buildings of the town, all the cheerful promise of habitation and civilisation before them.

Since their arrival in Wales, Nimue had felt like a snake, shedding its skin. The rain cleansed her, washed away the past, the years of her childhood and girlhood secure with her father in London. She had applied herself dutifully to earning her bed and board, running the house in Mary's place, doing all she could to ensure the other woman's comfort, assisting Gilbert if he requested it in transacting the business of the estate. He hardly spoke to her and when he did, it was in a brusque, almost offensive manner, but Nimue was aware of his inner conflicts and knew how he wrestled with himself when he was alone in his chamber. She was content that matters should be so, distanced between them. She did not love Gilbert, and she could never love him. She must be patient, trusting, and her father's prophecy would be fulfilled, her destiny would reveal itself.

As the days passed, she knew with increasing certainty that this land would some day give her her heart's desire, even if she must wait a hundred years for it to come to her. Over each tree, round each curve of the hill, in each cloud and shadow, there was a sense of something waiting, breath held, time suspended. Nimue did not question but waited with it, going quietly about the work of the house, letting the present moment have her and giving no thought for what might come.

It was obvious that Mary would never be happy applying herself to matters in the kitchen, the dairy, the yard. She would disdain to soil her pretty shoes going among the hens to find the eggs, and she was afraid of the goat. She preferred to sit in the warmth of the parlour, stitching at her uneven sampler, her mind filled with sharp, though shallow, schemes. She would not polish nor prepare fowl or fish for the oven. She was not interested in the herbs and simples of the stillroom, in the tasks a lady must undertake for her household.

Mary was cast in higher mould, Nimue told herself with an inward smile, born to be waited on, to be decorative and ornamental for her lord and to be the focus of employment for others. The sooner the better, then, that she found herself a husband before her disposition soured and her sweetness curdled. Although, Nimue knew what her father would have said if told of the spells Mary was anticipating. She could almost hear his bellow of amusement.

'Will the woman make you into a hedge witch, Nimue? Or will she have you conjure a demon in the smoke? Keep to the light, child, and you will see all clearly.'

Nimue had kept her own counsel since their arrival, and she revealed little in response to Mary's curious questioning about her powers. She had been non-commital, and claimed only that, like her father, she could plot the positions of the stars and planets and draw up a chart.

Once, when she and her father had been in Southwark, they had seen the crowd of housewives, goodbodies and men who were fond fathers stirred by just a few words to attack a witch, led by a girl with a sullen face who had been disappointed in love. The woman – young and swan-necked, with her slender body clumsy from the child she carried – had been newly-widowed, it seemed, and though her skin was pearly soft and luminous, her eyes were black-ringed with grief. Beneath the taunts of the crowd she had run helplessly, pulling her baby by the hand, so that it fell and its thin wails of hurt were like cobwebs quivering on the air above the growl of the crowd's fearful glee and growing delight in their sport. There had been a young boy, too, who had tried to keep them from his mother, and then, seeing her run with the little girl, had bent to gather the witch's familiar in his arms. It was a small brindled cat, whose wide eyes stared and ears pricked over the boy's shoulder, until a stone hit it.

They had escaped at last, and it had been Gereint Gwynne who had taken them from the street into his small house, sat the distraught woman down before the fire and soothed the crying child. Nimue had brought food and wine, salves for their bruises, and patiently fed the little cat scraps as the boy watched, hovering impotently, until it began at last to wash its face and purr through the bloody fur on its nose. With money Gereint gave them, the small party had disappeared like an unexpected and uneasy dream lost, into the night and Nimue never saw them again.

But she had never forgotten how a woman's spite, and the ignorance of cloddish minds had turned the familiar, bustling afternoon into a baiting, but of a helpless woman and two children rather than a bear or a bull.

'They will destroy what they do not understand,' Gereint Gwynne had said, his eyes dark. 'They would destroy their Redeemer anew if he walked on the water of the Thames tomorrow, Nimue.' And she knew intuitively that he was right.

Flint in the rain was a huddle of dripping houses, horses, faces beneath hoods, light and glimpses of fires, the sighing and soughing of the soft Welsh tongue. She warmed herself gratefully as she waited at the house where Llew took her while the letter was read, and accepted the wine that was proffered with instinctive hospitality to a young and comely visitor. The fact that she was never going to achieve the status of Mistress of Grannah as Gilbert's wife did not seem to matter, in this country of poets and princes gallantry was assured by her very appearance, and in spite of her lowly position as an assumed dependent of the Stoneyathes and her plain gown and cloak she was gratifyingly aware that men turned, drawn, to look at her. Some covertly, some openly. But yes, they looked, and on this day of adventure, Nimue responded with the artless pleasure of a child, her feminine soul tingling in the awareness of her power.

They had purchases to make, provisions to get which were loaded upon Llew's mount, and, hungry, they bought pasties and beer at an inn, enjoying the unaccustomed pleasures of a town even in the rain. At last, with the reply from Ignatius Smith carefully folded, safely stowed beneath her cloak, their ponies rested, she and Llew set off along the road that would lead them back to Grannah.

The afternoon was darkening into a rain-torn evening, with blusters of misty showers driving into her face, and they were walking the beasts beneath trees that reached pillars of blackness above the path when Llew reined in his mount and pointed.

Nimue turned her head.

'What is it?'

'Pendragon,' was the reply, and the boy crossed himself, the movement of his hand a pale blur. There was a break in the trees, and beyond them, she saw a hill and a tower gaunt against the racing sky, with silvery light behind it where the cloud broke. And there was something else, something that set her pulses quickening. In the dimness, a white horse was waiting quietly, neck bent to crop the grasses, looking as though it could not be real.

Nimue had heard by this time the servants' stories of the wizard Merlin Pendragon, but she had said no more about her encounter with the man who had ridden seemingly from the sea, preferring to keep her silence. But she was burning with curiosity as to his identity. If he was called Merlin and could curse as fluently as her father in the names of certain spirits and demons, almost certainly he was some sort of wizard, but it could not be the ancient who had terrified the townsfolk and country people at Michaelmas fairs and who, according to what Jonas Mowas had revealed during a further call at Grannah, had relieved many a swollen-faced sufferer of his teeth, pulling them out in full view of the assembled populace to the howls of the afflicted. Nimue wondered briefly whether this colourful figure was so proficient in magic that he could renew his youth, so that when he rode abroad it was not as an old man but as the dark warrior she had seen between sea and sky in the moonlight.

There was a glimmer of light somewhere at the foot of the tower, and a track of sorts leading to it. The silver cloud had turned now to pewter, and Nimue felt her curiosity – and something else she could not name – draw her towards the path, though the lad shook his head and said something in the Welsh tongue, his eyes wide with fright, when she turned her pony's head.

'I will go. If you are afraid, wait here for me,' she instructed him coolly, a strange decision settling over her mind. It was at Pendragon tower that she would find the answers to her questions about the man who had ridden the white horse, and already her pony's feet were treading the track between the trees as though it knew the way forward. Nimue felt sudden wild anticipation thrill through her, making her blood race in her veins.

'Wait,' she repeated, and the boy nodded a trifle sullenly, though he looked relieved that he was not to be pressed to accompany her.

The pony trod the dark path sure-footedly, and Nimue slid from its back in a kind of yard beside a dim doorway, and tethered it to a ring in the wall. Pulling her cloak about her, she hesitated for a moment, feeling suspended between the earth and the cloud-racked sky above and around her, into which the tower reached a groping finger. There were scents assailing her nostrils, sharp and bitter herb smells as well as the deep mysterious fragrance of the woods, with their mould and decay, secret glimpses of life and death. A moment between the past and the future. She breathed deeply, then breaking the trance she knocked hard upon the door with the handle of her crop.

She did not know what to expect, and her anticipation was heightened by an awareness of the forbidden. There was no sign of life however, no movement, and her heart began to shrink in disappointment. She had not realised how much she had wanted to see him again, how he had invaded her mind and haunted the edges of her dreams, dark on the whiteness of his mount. Then, suddenly the door was pulled open and she saw the outline of a man's figure blurred against firelight beyond, and the light of candles.

'Who knocks?' demanded a deep voice.

'I would speak with the wizard,' Nimue said, breathlessly clasping her hands together beneath her cloak to stop them from trembling, though whether it was with fear or excitement, she did not know. 'I have been told that he has the power to look into the future. I would know what it holds for me.'

To her surprise there was a silence, and she was aware that eyes were studying her closely. Then, as her heart pounded in her throat, the deep voice said in tones that were far from cordial:

'Oh, I see it is the much-travelled Mistress Gwynne. From London. The lady who holds her head higher than Mistress Mary Stoneyathe, and who can keep silence, unlike most of the rest of her sex. What are you doing summoning the dark powers at my wild tower, Mistress Gwynne? Have you not powers of your own, witch?'

'No,' she said, taken aback at this onslaught, surprised too that the wizard should know her name and so much about her. 'At least, I – I cannot tell.' Confusion swept over her, uncertainty as to how to answer, and the sense of anti-climax brought sudden tiredness heavy to her limbs. She took a firmer grip on her crop, and another deep breath, something impelling her to add:

'I do not know - if my future is here, if I will find my heart's desire, if this is where I belong.' She hesitated, then still impelled to speak, went on in a low voice: 'I believe you are wise. Can you advise me?'

Again there was a silence, and the shadow in the doorway seemed to be considering, leaning coolly against the thick wood with arms folded. He was tall and his face pulled back out of the light. Nimue tried to make out his features, but could not, only a thick mass of hair that fell to his shoulders. Was this the man who rode the white horse? Or was it the ancient, transformed by magic? The firelight behind him flickered and her senses began to swim.

Fire. She saw it again, the flames leaping up into the dark sky, the timbers exploding fiercely in white-hot charred ash, and she heard again the voice that wailed in the night wind. As she swayed, lost in the vision, she realised that it was her own voice, that she was speaking the words aloud:

'My love, my love, my love.'

A hand seized her wrist, twisting it so that she gasped, and another turned her chin up to the light.

'Who are you?' the man from the sea hissed above her, and there was an arm, unyielding as iron, round her shoulders, holding her so that she did not fall. 'A pensioner of Stoneyathe I hear, a woman whose father left her nothing but his powers – but what were his powers? What do you see when you look into the dark that makes you call me in your trance, to call me your love?'

Nimue could feel the warmth of his lean hand on her arm even through the folds of her cloak and she had become strangely light-headed, as though she might float away if he let her go.

'I see danger,' she heard her own voice saying. 'If you are the one, take care. There is fire and death. Beware the fire. I would save you if I could, but I am not skilled in these arts, I do not know whether my power is strong enough.'

Another silence, vibrating with sound, and then he took his arms away and let her go with a sudden guffaw of amusement, as he had done at her spirited retort in the moonlight beside the sea.

'Not strong enough? You?' he said, and turned into the doorway, still laughing. He disappeared for a moment, then returned quickly and placed something in her hands, closing her fingers round the hard surface.

'Go,' he said, low and harsh, no laughter now, and she found herself leaning towards him, straining to meet his eyes. He pulled back his head so that his face was once more in shadow and half-hidden by his black hair. 'This is not the time. We will meet again, you and I.'

Then, as she hesitated, still light-headed from his closeness and the intensity of her vision, he turned her none too gently away from him and pushed her into the dark evening where her pony was moving impatiently, and beyond the trees, Llew waited. Silently, she mounted from the edge of a water-trough that glimmered in the half-light, and clucked her tongue to the beast without looking back. She was aware of a tingling between her shoulder-blades, making her want to shrug them. She knew that he watched from his tower until she had passed into the shadows beneath the trees and together with Llew, was long gone from his sight.

When they returned to Grannah, tired and hungry, Nimue found that there had been a visitor in her absence. Indeed, the erring daughter of Caercerrig, Dorabella Mowas, was now enthroned in the parlour where the best candles were burning brightly, plucking with long white fingers at the strings of the Celtic harp and singing in husky, strangely sexless tones, while Gilbert listened, seemingly entranced, his head on his hand beside her. Mary, at a little distance, was watching with some calculation. It was obvious that she had not yet made up her mind what her attitude to this newcomer was to be.

When Nimue entered the parlour, Dorabella stopped ostentatiously in mid-phrase, her hands arrested in the air, staring with the almost offensive disregard of a young child – or, Nimue thought irritated in spite of herself, someone who might indeed learn manners from the beatings her father was too soft to give her – as Gilbert somewhat stiffly made introductions. But she was no child, Nimue could see that at a glance. She was a woman grown, though her features were clear and artless, untouched by the cares of responsibility. But the expression in her pale eyes increased Nimue's initial irritation.

'I have heard of you, you are the witch,' she stated reprovingly, a remark to which Nimue did not feel called upon to reply. Instead she held out her letter to Gilbert, with the pointed comment:

'Since I am very tired, I will retire with your permission.'

He seemed confused, and as though her presence made him uneasy. Nimue, watching him, supposed rather cynically that even he felt ashamed that his discarded bride was placed in the position of servant while a new light o' love invaded the parlour.

'No, stay, Dorabella is entertaining us most beautifully. She arrived earlier and has been benighted – the weather has worsened, I think.'

Nimue thought it best not to point out that she had been riding through the very same weather for hours, and sat down composedly.

'As you wish.'

'Sing on,' Gilbert directed, turning back to Dorabella, and the girl curled her fingers once again across the strings, so that a shiver of sound cascaded like water into the room. As she sang, in the light flat voice that was so different to Jonas Mowas's mellifluous tones, Nimue studied her. Slim, young, in a plain gown of brown cloth trimmed with velvet, with a rosary at her

41

waist. She had almost the appearance of a holy sister, emphasised by the way her wheat-coloured hair was drawn back beneath her brown cap. Her face was pale and had an intense light about it.

'A fanatic,' Nimue thought with sudden insight, and she shivered involuntarily, partly from her tiredness and partly from a sense of foreboding. Her father had always warned her to beware of fanaticism in all its forms. He remembered as a youth seeing the fires at Smithfield blazing by the order of the obsessed Queen Mary, trying to make England Catholic for the Spanish Philip.

'No God of power needs blood,' he had said on many occasions. 'The powerful do not need to inspire fear. Their strength comes from the with-holding of their hand.'

But if Nimue found Dorabella Mowas's intensity rather disturbing, it was obvious that Gilbert did not. He was watching her with an absorption that made Nimue's mouth curl slightly. A new light o' love indeed, and so much for his mad escapade to ask her father for her own hand in marriage. It struck her that Gilbert had the misfortune to be drawn irresistibly to women who were in their way stronger than he, and then he found himself fighting to free himself from their strength. But perhaps he would find happiness with Dorabella, though, dispassionately examining the hard lines of the girl's cheek and jaw bones beneath the soft skin, she doubted it. Life with Dorabella, she suspected, would be like wearing a hair shirt.

The Welsh girl was not quite as unsubtle as she seemed, however. The song over, she rose and came to Mary, bending over her solicitously, her flat voice infused with concern.

'Forgive me, madam. I had forgotten you were an invalid, and it is very late. I will assist you to your bed and help you to sleep.'

Gratification dawned in Mary's sharp little face, as well as surprise at being cast as ailing dowager, and she threw a look of triumph towards Nimue, who was trying not to nod from weariness and the heat of the parlour on her low stool. Nimue did not see it, but Gilbert was on his feet immediately.

'Certainly not Dorabella, you are our honoured guest. Mary is quite capable of getting to her room without your assistance.'

Dorabella turned her pale face slowly towards him, and Nimue knew that he was lost.

'I have always loved this house,' she said, her strange tones spreading like a net, a trap, through the chamber, though it was Gilbert, transfixed and staring, who was the helpless prey she stalked. 'And I loved your cousin David, he was a saint, nothing less, and an inspiration to those around him. I hope that I might come to be regarded as something more than a guest in your household, in time, Gilbert.'

'I would be glad of your arm, Dorabella,' Mary made haste to declare, in a far-away tone of suffering patiently borne. 'And your voice is sweet, I am sure it would help me to sleep if you were to sing to me in my chamber. I have longed often for a sister to cherish, with whom to share secrets.'

Triumphantly, ignoring Gilbert's expression of mingled fascination and horror at this careless indiscretion, she allowed herself to be assisted from the parlour, and even in her weariness and irritation, Nimue was hard put not to laugh out loud. She managed to restrain herself, however, and when Mary had been escorted with solicitude to the door, and up the stairs, she once again asked Gilbert's permission to retire, keeping her manner quietly noncommital. As though relieved, he made no attempt this time to keep her, and she took her candle and climbed the stairs to shut herself in her chamber, away from the soft high chattering, like that of baby birds, in Mary's room – Mary herself doing most of the talking.

Mary, Nimue thought, her cynicism extending from Gilbert to encompass his sister as she sat trying to calm her mind after the events of the day, turning them over to examine them quietly and make her peace with them, had also been an eager convert.

But what of herself, had she too not suffered a sea-change and lost her soul to another? Tonight she had encountered someone who, if he was not the wizard Merlin, nevertheless had the ability to weave himself into the dangerous webs of her future and had the power to cast such a spell upon her that she knew in her secret heart that if he ever called her, she would go to him without knowing why – and even without yet having seen his face clearly.

Sitting in the quiet of her chamber, reliving those brief moments between the firelight of Pendragon tower and the night outside its door, the pressure of his arms and voice, the touch of his fingers, the moving shadows, gleams and hidden promises in the urgency of his presence, she took from her cloak the object he had pressed into her hands, and examined it in the light of the candle.

It was a ring, of some heavy tarnished metal, silver she supposed, into which was set a round gem that swam like pale translucent water in the soft flame.

Her father had instructed her in the secrets and meaning of gems, though many of them she had never seen, being no Elizabeth to flaunt it before her courtiers in the glory of emeralds, rubies, pearls, and the treasures cast at her feet in tribute by the wealth of the New Indies. But as Nimue stared slowly into the depths of the ring, her father's voice seemed to echo in her ears.

'It is a moonstone, Nimue, the stone of the goddess, mistress of the night. All crystals and stones hold power, and everything upon the earth a living force. The moonstone is for the woman in you, no longer a child, but a woman whose tides reach as wide and as deep as the tides pulled by the moon. Never fear, you can wear it for your strength too is as deep as the ocean, fathomless.'

She seemed to feel those depths beneath her feet, lifting her. Her father had spoken to her many times of the secret power of the feminine, and she had not understood then. But now, as she turned the ring over in her fingers, recalling the touch of the hands which had closed her own round the jewel, she knew why she needed to be strong. It was not for herself only, it was also for him. The man from the sea. The man with the dark shadowed face. Her fate and destiny and true love.

4

A stippled evening, streaks of light in the west, when a horseman came trotting slowly into the yard, and the dogs set up their usual clamorous barking. Nimue was in the kitchen with Morfydd, her gown enveloped in a rough apron of sacking, for the two women and the girls who served in the house had been plucking and preparing fowl, geese and pigeon for the making of festive pies and pasties. Already there had been a great roasting and boiling and making of broths and jellies against the winter months. Salted bacon and hams, venison and mutton, hung in the smokehouse and the larder, and for all that Mary bemoaned the lack of ready money to purchase luxuries, the household would not starve.

Flushed from the heat of the fire, her eyes luminous and her soft curls in smudges round her face where she had reached up impatiently to push them back, Nimue was summoned by the excited words, 'English it is, mistress, wanting you,' and she hurried out into the hall where the great door stood open, and a broadshouldered figure with a swagger that was only a little dulled by weariness, was impatiently awaiting her. She cried out in surprise and pleasure.

'Why, Will!'

And it was indeed Will Shakespeare himself, wrapped in a heavy dark blue cloak, and with lines of fatigue shadowing his face, but the curling black hair and devil-have-'em eyes swept her immediately into another time, and another place. He smiled at the sight of her, bringing all the vivid life of London with him, and the remembrances flooded over Nimue of long nights sitting quietly in her corner, absorbed, while he discoursed on all things under the sun with her father and the candles burned low, scenting the room with bayberry, and at last the dawn rose over the sleeping city. She bit her lip, recalling memories too of laughter at his extravagant compliments to his host's 'fair wench, the Dark Lady of my dreams'.

'Gereint, your daughter is a witch, she has stolen my heart light-fingered as a street urchin, and all the time sitting there with a face like a closeted saint, filled with secrets.'

'I thought your wife held your heart,' Nimue retorted, her eyes sparkling, but Will Shakespeare was not deterred, and sketched an ardent actor's mime of passion.

'She has my everyday heart, it is true, oh fair divinity, but you have my high day, holyday heart, which I have kept secret until it was needed. Holyday hearts are frail things, they cannot survive the workaday round. I make you a present of mine, will you tear it apart in your dainty fingers, sweet mistress? Pity a poor playwright who must deal in dreams.'

Nimue was laughing and Gereint's look amused.

'I will go to Stratford, to Anne and tell her,' the girl declared pertly. 'She cares for your children while you follow rainbows – and pretty women. Think shame, Will Shakespeare.'

'Anne does not want my holyday heart, coz. They are uncomfortable things. And as for rainbows, she would be glad of the crock of gold at the end of them, to eke out the miserly earnings of her ne'er-do-well thespian husband. But perhaps you will inspire me to write a new play that will touch the heart of the Queen, and make my fortune. The name of William Shakespeare is written in the stars, scrawled across the sky, is it not, Gereint?'

'Chance would be a fine thing,' teased Nimue, while Gereint lolled easily in his great chair, smiling.

And now here was Will himself, no figure from the past but real enough, standing before her in the shadowed evening light of the hall at Grannah, with the same boisterous laughing look in his eyes. Will mocked at life, she had never seen him anything but merry. Nimue, her face alight with delight, forgot her workaday garb and her bloodied hands and went forward impulsively, catching up his fists in their worn, gauntleted leather.

'Will, where in heaven's name have you come from? Have you ridden far, you must be exhausted. And hungry.'

'I could swallow a draught of ale,' he admitted and, flushing, she called Morfydd to bring him some refreshment, then shook her head at him, her eyes dancing, her joy shining in her face.

'I do not believe it. This is some impish trick. It cannot be you. You are in London, a lifetime away.'

'Oh, I was. But the god who rules my destiny wagged his finger in a northerly direction, so now I am touring in the wilderness, and in Chester with my lord Stanley's 'cry of players',' he informed her, and as Morfydd appeared, plump and beaming, he took the cup of ale she proffered and drained it thirstily. 'Ah, this gives a man new life. The city makes us welcome, but I braved the roads and the weather to venture into wild Wales to find my Dark Lady, to congratulate the bride of Stoneyathe.' And, suddenly serious, he gave her a long, appraising look. 'Is it well, Nimue? That rash marriage, how goes it, girl? Are you happy?'

But it was the afternoon of the following day, on the seashore in the shadow of Flint Castle, before she could answer him. It had not been possibly to talk privately at Grannah. Gilbert and Mary had seized and monopolised the visitor from London, sweeping him into the parlour to sit hours hungrily hanging upon his words as though he had arrived from another world, wanting to hear the Court gossip, and how life still went in the city. On the surface, as they sat together they seemed to make apparent good company. Gilbert was gracious, Mary decked out hastily in her finery for the occasion – and the prospect of a man of sophistication, versed in the ways of the world, captive in the parlour to admire her. Nimue sat glowing with quiet pleasure on a low stool as she watched Will's volatile change of expression, he detailing some scandal and making them all laugh.

The household at Grannah could not have been more harmonious. But Will, with his acuteness and awareness, could tell that matters were not as straightforward as they seemed. He sensed the undercurrents in the atmosphere, and it was obvious from Nimue's ringless hand that she and Gilbert were not yet wedded.

But under Gilbert's roof both Will and Nimue felt themselves constrained and it was on the wide wet sands, with the hills softly gathering themselves together inland and the expanse of the glittering estuary before them catching points of light, that she told him of what had come of that hasty match entered into at her father's deathbed. She told him too of her meeting with the white horse and its rider on the seashore, and of her visit to Pendragon tower. And of how he had given her the moonstone, and of her certainty that she had found the destiny her father had foreseen.

'Yes, I am happy here, Will, because I think I have come where I was meant to be,' she said, her eyes following the line of the light to the horizon. 'Oh, I do not know who he is, nor when we shall meet again, and I have yet to see his face clearly, but I am content to wait. He is what he is, but he is my fate, and where he is, that is where my future lies. I would not leave Grannah now, for all that I live by cold charity, earning my bed and board because Gilbert chooses to let me. Nor because Gilbert will probably marry Dorabella Mowas and she is

48

dangerous. She has the eyes of a fanatic, and believes that I possess the dark powers of a witch.'

'Hmm,' Will muttered, into the wind, as they walked slowly along the sands together. In the inn behind them, within the gates of Flint Town itself, Llew was seeing to their mounts, Will's horse and Nimue's pony, and his own. The tidal waters of the estuary that covered the reaches of Flint Sands and lapped at the busy stones of the port where ships cowered, black shapes against the quay, spread wide, glittering, and the sky threatened snow.

'A strange uneasy sort of happiness, girl,' Will commented darkly. 'I do not share your faith in the goodness of human nature. You must protect yourself. Your father was content to wander among the clouds but he would not have wanted you to lack while you too tread those realms. Love and fate and destiny are all very well, bravely spoken, but they are tender plants that need nurturing, and when the frost comes, then they die. Come back with me to London. I will find you a place - .'

'Oh, Will. A serving wench? A tavern doxy?' Her light teasing voice robbed the words of their sting. 'You forget, I have a place. I am Mary's pensioner now, and she is afraid to cross me in case she will lose the fine husband she has marked for herself. It is their cousin David's man of business, and now their own. He has his finger in all the pies at Grannah, and can speak English as silver-tongued as my lord Dudley himself, who my father told me would play pretty Robin to the Queen. His name is Ignatius Smith, and she has set her mind on him though he is greying and she is not turned twenty. Oh, it is not his person she desires but his money and his house here in Flint with a garden and orchard that takes her fancy, and a position in society where she can queen it over the local gentry. Mary was born to queen it over the rest and if Dorabella comes to Grannah as Gilbert's wife it will be like a spark to tinder, there is no room for them both.'

'And what then will become of you?' he fretted. 'For your father's sake, Nimue - .'

She turned into the wind that came in clean from the sea, shrugging. 'It was my father who sent me here, Will. He saw my fate. And I think Gilbert will not turn me out, for all his faults he is proud of his honour, and he gave his word. And - .' She paused, the fingers of the wind plucking at her hood and bringing the dusky colour stinging to her cheeks. 'There is Pendragon.'

He pulled the dark blue folds of his cloak tighter round him, turning to look back at the towers of Flint. She saw with some surprise that there was a heaviness to him that rested ill on one born to nature's bounty, to whom life came easily. When he spoke, the words seemed dragged from him, paining his throat to speak them.

'Has it come to this, then? I can see in your face that I have lost you, you have gone from me, girl.'

'Will, you never had me,' Nimue said, turning to face him, startled into a challenge she did not mean, a coolness and bluntness of speech that would hurt him afterwards.

'Was there nothing, then, between us? Deny it if you dare,' he said fiercely, beneath his breath. 'You are my Dark Lady, my shadow leaping ahead of me to guide my feet. Ah, Nimue, have pity girl.'

But from somewhere, she found the courage to tell him the truth. She had been unaware herself, nostalgic for the past, but when the words left her lips she knew them for wisdom given to her from some hidden source she had not known before, deep within her.

'I was a child then, back in that other world, whatever there was between us was a game between children, a tale like your strutting on the stage. Now I am a woman, and I have found my soul mate, dark and brooding though he is and strange to me. I can be nothing to you, Will. My destiny lies with him for better or for worse, whatever it brings to me, whether love or death.'

Tense against the shining sea, they faced each other like Spanish duellists. Then Will reached out and touched the black curls that tendrilled around her face, blowing in the wind. He spoke very gently, looking into her eyes.

'Yet it might have been me - ,' he began, but she interrupted, turning her head stiffly away from the touch of his fingers, afraid she would give way to him.

'No, never, Will, never. You were a dear friend, you will always be dear to me, but you have a wife and children. You know and I know that you can never forget that. And,' she added, with a sudden flash of insight, 'It is not me that you want, your Dark Lady though I may be, it is something apart from me. Your vision, your inspiration, Will. You follow your fate as I do, and you must go where it leads. It is not any woman on earth but an enchantment that you cannot escape.'

'Perhaps,' he muttered, turning away also. 'But you are my enchantment, I would warm myself with your laughter, girl, those many nights when we sat, the three of us, watching for the dawn. Only a child, yes, but your father knew, he knew you were more than a child to me.'

'My father trusted you,' Nimue said simply.

'I am only a working man, a jobbing actor,' he replied, with a gesture. 'I write plays, I am a craftsman not a philosopher. The world is all a stage to me, and the fate of each human being just one more tale to please the groundlings who watch with their mouths open and cry 'Mercy' and 'Pity' and in the next breath, 'Vengeance' and 'Death'. But sometimes, as in your father's company and yours those nights beside the hearth, roaming the great wastes of time and space, conjuring the power of the mind, I am above myself, I see visions beyond the technicalities and the words.'

Seeing the expression on her face, he checked himself then went on in a different tone. 'Here, for instance, at Flint, there is a play, waiting for me to write it. I thought of it when I set out into the wilds from Chester to find you, and now, in the shadow of the towers, with you at my arm's length and yet gone far from me, the words I have half-heard come tumbling over themselves into my mind.'

'A play?' Nimue queried, glad that he seemed to have turned his hungry attention from her to generalities. 'What play?'

'A betrayal,' he said, and there was bleakness in his voice. 'A betrayal at this very castle, in this base court, where kings – and queens, Nimue, and queens – grow base.'

'Tell me,' Nimue said, coolly distant. She knew that he deluded himself, and that in shame he would want to forget what had passed between them in these moments once they had gone.

'There was a Richard of England came here also to await his fate,' Will was saying, his eyes brooding, turned inward. 'He stood on these tattered battlements watching as the usurper Bolingbroke came along the seashore with all his host. A man in torment, longing for the end.' He began to speak quietly, words that Nimue felt stab home to her heart like knives.

What must the king do now? Must he submit?
The king shall do it: must he be deposed?
The king shall be contented; must he lose
The name of king? o' God's name, let it go:
I'll give my jewels for a set of beads,
My gorgeous palace for a hermitage,
My gay apparel for an almsman's gown,
My figured goblets for a dish of wood,
My sceptre for a palmer's walking-staff,
My subjects for a pair of carved saints,
And my large kingdom for a little grave,
A little little grave, an obscure grave; -
Or I'll be buried in the king's highway,
Some way of common trade, where subjects' feet
May hourly trample on their sovereign's head.

Then without another word and without looking at Nimue, he turned and began to walk back towards the towers of Flint, and she followed slowly behind him.

Ever since that first dark evening's encounter with the man from the sea at forsaken Pendragon, Nimue had taken to stopping at her work and dreaming over the pale depths of her moonstone, in the courtyard while she carried in the milk from the goat, or in the tangled grasses searching for wild mushrooms beside the bleak and empty traceries of the guelder rose, shaken in the wind, or alone in her chamber when the business of the day was done. Her fate was already decided, but she would not be a mope and give herself up to profitless fancy. Her father had believed that each carved out his destiny with the tools he was given, and had advised her often, 'Do not wait for things to happen, Nimue. Make them happen yourself.' So though she longed for some sign from Pendragon, none came and she wantonly sought for a reason why she must go to him and pass by the tower again.

Whatever she had stored within her heart to say to him, she would not, for shame's sake, ride so far without a legitimate errand, and chance played into her hand when Will Shakespeare declined Gilbert's casual invitation to accept the hospitality of Grannah, explaining that he must return to Chester and my lord of Derby's town house to join the players on the morning immediately following his arrival, but laughingly declaring that he would appreciate a civilised bed to snore to himself for that night, since he must share with both the 'wenches' as the company travelled, and they, lisping their parts and their affairs hours together, distracted his nights worse than any woman.

Nimue announced composedly that she would take Llew with her and ride with her old friend for part of the way to give him Godspeed, in spite of Mary's shriek and shudder, giving Will an apologetic feminine flutter of dainty hands as she denounced the weather prettily as 'too, too dreadful for a lady to venture out, I swear.' Gilbert shrugged and said she must of course do as she pleased, but added that if she was to ride as far as Flint, she might do him a service by delivering a letter to Ignatius Smith, his man of business, summoning him to Grannah.

On hearing this, Mary roused herself vivaciously from her cocoon of shawls and begged Nimue to deliver a letter also to Ignatius Smith's sister, Mistress Emma Smith, requesting the instructions for making Welshcakes, as she was resolved to become a true Welshwoman.

This, Nimue knew, was for Ignatius Smith's benefit not for the approval of his sister. As she told Will while they stood on the windswept sands, Mary had set her cap at the darkly stocky, no longer youthful lawyer within an hour of his appearance when he had first called at Grannah to discuss the affairs of the estate with Gilbert. It was doubtful whether his physical appearance would ever have roused even a spark of ardour in Mary's breast, kindling her firm determination to have him, but she had heard from the gossip which she somehow managed to conduct with Morfydd and Llew and the other servants (who hardly spoke the English tongue) that Mister Smith was far more prosperous than most of the gentry round about because he had had the foresightedness to speculate in many dubious trading enterprises, particularly those risky ventures in the New World, to which the Queen had herself turned a blind eye in private while she admonished her captains, Raleigh, Drake and the like, in public.

Nimue had been surprised to encounter such cosmopolitan shrewdness across the Marches of Wales, and Mary had been frankly filled with admiring approval of Mister Smith's enterprise. What had helped to fan the flames of her passion was not, however, the fact that Mister Smith had never married, had long lived a bachelor life with his sister and was thus overdue for a woman to tease and torment him, so might fall an easy prey to her matrimonial toils. It was something else.

When he arrived, he had been smitten by her charms in as obvious a manner as many another of his sex, but he had also been at pains to declare himself captivated by her sparkling wit and conversation. To be admired for her mind was a situation Mary had never before encountered, and she found it most gratifying, since she could feel herself equal, if not superior, to those cool, clever women like Nimue and Dorabella Mowas, who made her feel strangely disquieted, though she could not for the life of her have explained why.

Discussion concerning the business of the estate and matters of interest appertaining to it kept Ignatius Smith and Gilbert closeted through the whole of one forenoon in the winter parlour which cousin David had made his own sanctum and which contained, amongst other things, relics of the eccentric's successful campaigns waged against the bear and bull baiting fraternity and habitues of cock fights and the hunting field. Spurs torn from the legs of birds, with the blood still upon them, kept pride of place with the collars of bears and chains removed from bulls. A collection of hunting horns was mounted above the fireplace, together with a couple of broken swords and a crossbow. Quite what the significance of that was, no-one had been able to tell the new master of the house.

The discussions were laid aside while Mister Smith and Gilbert joined the ladies for dinner, but later, the lawyer having departed, and sitting in the parlour in the evening bearing a petulant Mary company, Gilbert had begun to talk in cautious, calculating tones, exploring ideas Ignatius Smith's conversation had put into his head. There was a gleam in his eye that Nimue regarded with growing disquiet, though Mary was too absorbed in plans of how she might best entrap the lawyer to notice. She wondered aloud, addressing her remarks to no-one in particular, and speculating idly as to whether, since his house was a ride away in Flint Town, any love potion that Nimue might be good enough to concoct for her schemes might work if it was effected at a distance – both the potion itself and the effects of which, Nimue pointedly refused to discuss.

Gilbert had in the first flush of exhilaration at the prospect of his inheritance, cared nothing about interesting himself in the details of how best to scrape a day-to-day living from his acquired estates. He had spent too many years existing from day to day, seizing the opportunity as it presented itself to him and avoiding long-term commitments. In addition, his temperament and his sister's had been honed by their circumstances to a fine disregard for honest toil and a conviction that appearances were all – at Court, it was often the case that 'fine feathers made fine birds', though the birds themselves might be on the point of extinction.

Consequently the thought of applying himself to making his estate prosper, even the thought of soiling his hands, that were so elegant when handling cards and dice in company, or even strumming a lute – such pastimes having previously often been a means to obtaining his bread and butter – did not noticeably figure very largely in Gilbert's mind. He would be the land-owner but he would let others work the land, such humble toiling being the natural lot of those of the lower orders who were accustomed to such a way of existence, those born, as some undoubtedly were, to serve their betters.

He himself he fiercely, though privately, envisioned as being free for the first time in his life to indulge himself to the full in whatever pursuits he could discover in the neighbourhood to satisfy him. The prospect of ornamenting society in the parish and the county as Stoneyathe of Grannah, rather than the worried pensioner of the state who had in the past – now happily gone for good – anxiously counted the holes in his hose at their lodging off Cheapside, and been driven to lining his Court shoes with straw, had seemed all that he required for the moment from the beneficent providence which had so dazzlingly chosen to smile upon him.

But he discovered when he arrived at Grannah that the land itself, the rocks and hills and woods that were now his own, from the deep earth to the soaring flight of eagles in the thin air above his head, held him in an unexpectedly passionate embrace. Gilbert would never truly love a woman, his nature was too filled with tortuous impulses, causing him to first advance and then retreat, and he could trust no-one in the world, he had learned, only himself and what he might hold in his own two hands. But he could love these acres of wild country, of which he was now, so unbelievable, the master. And as he rode the streaming wet ways with the men who had worked for his cousin David, and who accepted him without question as the latest in the line of men of Grannah – though Stoneyathe was not the name David and his father and grandfather had carried – Gilbert felt an almost ecstatic tumult of passions released within him.

This was all, this land that was his, and even as he sat with Ignatius Smith with the parchments, maps and documents of the estate before him, enquiring as to boundaries, tenancies, grazing and pastures, and all the teeming details his new existence must involve, his ambition, roused and fuelled beyond anything he had ever known in his life, was growing and multiplying like a rapacious weed spreading its roots within him.

It was not enough, he soon knew, to be master of Grannah. He must make Grannah great, he must marry and have sons, who would carry on his name. Gilbert had no desire for children for their own sake, and he did not realistically expect to love them. But they would be his, his property in the same way as the land – and in his mind's eye, he saw the grant of Grannah extending far beyond the boundaries that now marked it. A wife would be only a means by which he could found his dynasty, a new dynasty of Stoneyathe, his own creation.

It was not only Gilbert Stoneyathe who was so infected by this fever that shook men and tormented them and would not let them rest. All across the country there were wide expanses that were being enclosed in the name of the local lord and even the local yeoman, for all down to the lowest villein were reaching out and laying their claim to the earth which was no longer, it seemed, large enough for all. Gilbert, who had never previously felt it worth his while to consider such matters, owning nothing but the name of Stoneyathe, his family crest and the contents of the chest he kept hidden at the bottom of the press, began to speak of nothing else, at first covertly, then with increasing obsession.

Nimue watched the workings of his mind with apprehension, and some pity. She had known he was weak, but she was chilled to see that the new lord of Grannah, like many another before him, had fallen a prey to insatiable greed. Since he had come to Grannah, he would never rest, but all the lands west of the Severn and the Dee would not satisfy him now.

5

To Gilbert, who had been accustomed to seeing life in blacks and whites – though his conscience never ceased to struggle uncomfortably with the myriad shades of grey – it was all extremely simple. The land was there, and rightfully it belonged to Grannah, or more specifically, to him. All around the borders of the demesnes established long ago when life was much more casual, there were tracts of common lands where the peasantry had grazed their one cow and one goat each, allowed their scrawny fowl to wander, scratched their few yards of the common tillage. They behaved as though they had a right to it. Which, after a fashion, they had, through common usage long granted by the goodwill of their manorial lord and labour given in return, as well as service at arms if their lord summoned them to war.

Time out of mind, this was how things had always been.

In Wales especially, ancient history had not been created in settled towns, villages and peaceful manor houses. The tribes had lived, worked, fought and scraped their survival in a manner quite the opposite of domesticated, often travelling to winter and summer pastures, struggling with the land itself, where sometimes not even grazing could be wrestled from the rocks, the waters, the mountains. And as invader after invader attempted to enter the wild country, the Welsh had hunted in guerilla bands, never able to be pinned down, vanishing into the thick woods as noiselessly as they had come after wreaking havoc among the more solid ranks of soldiery and organised armies.

But with the eventual triumph of the English, it had been different. Lordships had been granted to favourites of the invading kings, great castles had sprung up that held the countryside in an iron grasp. Towns had been built, and settled by traders who spoke no Welsh, probably English or even French instead. Civilised urban living had established itself in places like Flint, as Ignatius Smith expansively explained to Gilbert. There on the windswept marshes of the Dee within the shelter of the town enclosure, guarded by its banks and ditches and the great town gates, protected by the towers of the castle, the taming of the land that had been fought over, picked over and seized by the strongest so that each new day had brought with it the need to watch for the sight of a fresh army, new men-at-arms, or even the yellow hair of the Norsemen who would attack from the sea and leave settlements razed and burning, at last began.

But inevitably, as the great lordships established themselves and the reforms in law and order encouraged the people to have confidence in the stability of living in more settled communities, more and more of the common land, land that from time immemorial had belonged to all or more realistically, to all who could seize and defend it, was swallowed up to swell such titles as Mortimer, de Braose, Fitzosbern. The Marches were in the hands of the still hated English and their sycophants and traitorous collaborators from end to end. As parts of the country were urbanised, little English towns blossomed while the Welsh for their part were driven to skulking outside their boundaries like savages and sometimes, as in the glorious days of Glyn Dwr, were forced to descend with fire and sword to take back their own meadows and pastures, hills and woods, streams and springs as well as their ancient rights and privileges. Justice was often sought not at the courts but at the point of a sword.

It did not work, though, and indeed, as Mister Smith declared with certainty, it could never work. Integration was the only answer. The Welsh, no more than any other race of peoples, must learn to live with their neighbours, and if those neighbours brought with them a system of urbanisation, settlement that integrated all and made them all accept the laws imposed upon the land, why, it was all to the good. In a settled society, a man could prosper. He himself, as he confided to Gilbert, had interests in London, and was able to live more than comfortably.

'Better than fighting wars, man,' he declared, unconsciously though less eccentrically echoing the precepts of cousin David. 'The Welsh have always been fighters, mind, and the best longbowmen they will always be. But in the proper place, in official service, see, with rates of pay, civilised, like. If we were still trying to keep the English out, where would we be now? Tearing ourselves and the country apart, I tell you. They are here to stay, that is what I firmly believe, and we can benefit from the situation, all of us. The Acts of Union, man, they were the best thing that ever happened to Wales, in my honest opinion, and I'd say the same to Ireland. Together we stand, united we fall, that is how it is, whether we like it or not.'

'A cool opportunist,' Nimue thought when she heard of Mister Smith's sentiments. But in its way that was no bad thing.

It was when opportunism was taken to extremes, when because of expediency or sheer greed, the hand that had already taken its fair share carried on taking at the expense of everyone else.

Her father's philosophy had been that there was enough for all, in moderation, and he had cast a sorry glance at the ways in which the new men, and those who had risen to swell the ranks of yeomen farmers, fresh to owning that half of the country that had changed hands after the church had lost it under Henry, were now in their greed trying to carve up the rest of Elizabeth's kingdom, in the rolling landscapes of Sussex and Kent and the green heartland of England as well as in the windswept hills of Wales.

Wales, always notorious in the days of the Tudor Henries, had only just begun to discover a sense of stability with the canny hand of Elizabeth guiding and encouraging the Council of Wales and the Marches. No longer, honest folk sighed in relief to reassure each other, was the Principality a land of outlaws and a safe haven for wrongdoers of all kinds. No more might desperate lawbreakers flee to freedom in the neighbouring holdings of the Marches, no longer were those in high places able to swagger openly as they lined their purses by dishonest means, hand in glove, many of them, with the myriad small smugglers and pirates who swarmed like hordes of troublesome insects in the little bays and creeks that fissured the coast, all of them making a mock of decent living.

Yet the growing class of small landowners, as well as the great lords, all who held land were still not satisfied. In an unprecedented atmosphere of land-fever, only partly the result of economic changes, tenants were being dispossessed, many in the wake of the monks and nuns of the previous generation, were being forced to take to the roads, homeless, and that word that rang hollow with doom, *enclosures*, was being pronounced with increasingly passionate vehemence in taprooms and in the kitchens of small farms and anywhere where men met and spoke to each other of the pressing affairs of the day.

61

The wild land, the common land, the rough high *ffridd* land, of which there were large areas round Grannah, might be enclosed by any landowner who had a mind, who could then claim it as his own, thus extending his property at the expense of freehold tenants and the rights of the lower classes. Gilbert was already making plans to enclose the high ground to the north and east of Grannah, and the long ridge of bony hills that ran down into the holdings of the Pendragon tower. It was no good for anything, hardly even for the sheep, Ignatius Smith had told him, rough land, rocks and scrub, but as part of the Grannah estates, it might yet prove its worth. Gilbert envisioned a fortune amassing itself without his having to do anything other than put up fences and claim the golden goose that would lay him golden eggs in due course. It was just a matter of time.

Nimue was not surprised to hear that Dorabella Mowas uncompromisingly applauded Gilbert's right to take any land he could. She baldly put forward the argument that if he did not take it, those lesser people, peasants and gipsies and the ignorant uncultured hordes of the native Welsh who by rights should not own land at all, since they did not know what to do with it, would soon occupy the whole of the country. Dorabella's pale eyes burned with all the fervour of the evangelist as she made her opinions known.

'Dada does not agree with me, of course, and neither did your cousin David, Gilbert. As I told you, he was too soft, too tolerant,' she declared, dismissing with a movement of an impatient hand the bounty of the master of Grannah and the honest ruminations of her father, who in his way had the good of all, high or low born, at heart, however he blustered and blasphemed around the subject. But Gilbert's cousin David was dead, and Jonas Mowas was not in the parlour at Grannah to defend himself, and his daughter went on with a glitter in her eyes which reflected that in Gilbert's.

'I am a good Christian, I believe in the importance of the individual, we are all reflections of God, however seemingly unworthy, and charity is the greatest of all the virtues. But those who know better, those who are enlightened and wise, must protect society from those who are not. They must defend their rights. There are too many low people, they spawn like toads and breed like rabbits.'

Her small, straight nose with its delicately chiselled nostrils was pinched in scorn and disgust, and Nimue felt a sense of revulsion at the girl's outpouring of bigoted cant, so thinly disguised as piousness.

'Who are they, these gipsies, these savages?' Dorabella was demanding, while the colour tinged her cheeks and Gilbert nodded his head in blind, dumb slavishness to her words. This kind of talk was meat and drink to him now.

'They have no sense of decency, no morals, and no feeling for the claims of others, those who have gained what they have by right,' said Dorabella, and Nimue, at the window, looking out into the late afternoon, could not help observing quietly:

'Perhaps they feel their birth, as natives of this country, gives them some claim.'

But Dorabella was unaware of subtlety.

'Natives, that is the word for them, yes. Like the native Irish, those filthy bog people, they cannot see that some are born to rule and others to obey. And they wander from place to place like the tribes of Israel, and settle anywhere they please, whether they have a right to do so or not. Why, Gilbert, they are a threat to all who own land. Dada cannot see this as you and I can.'

'Perhaps they do not know where to go, if they are homeless,' Nimue observed, recognising even as she spoke that her irritation was childish, but unable to stop the words from passing her lips. She addressed her remarks towards the view of the trees from the casement once again, and Mary, who never missed the opportunity to play the fine lady and who was watching from her seat beside the fire, gave a slight, puzzled frown. This afternoon there was something uncomfortable in the atmosphere, though she could not for the life of her identify what it was.

Dorabella brushed the interruption aside without an answer.

'There is a very old tradition in this countryside that if anyone can build a house within a night, so that there is a fire lit by morning in the hearth, they can claim the land to live on. *Ty unnos*, they call it, it means 'a house of one night',' she said.

'A house of one night,' Nimue could not help echoing, lingering over the words. Beyond the casement, the eternal Welsh rain, soft as the touch of the woolly sheep who brought prosperity to the uplands and clinging as the invisible webs of spiders, continued to pour from the leaden sky. 'It has a magical sound.'

Dorabella's pale, intense eyes regarded her intolerantly.

'It is squalid and sordid,' she pronounced. 'There is nothing magical about it at all. The main requirement is to get a fire burning, so the chimney has to be got up, but the rest of the building is often no better than a hovel. And these people will live in such conditions. It is practises like this that defile the land, upset the natural order which a good landlord tries so hard to maintain. But of course, so long as people like Dada and your cousin David will turn a blind eye to the fact that there is no real claim here, so long as the land can pass into the hands of this sort of irresponsible settler, rather than into the care of those who understand such matters, these people will continue to get away with it.'

'Perhaps,' Nimue suggested, a soft voice from the window, 'they have no choice.'

Once more Dorabella ignored her. She addressed Gilbert.

'My father is soft, but what good has it done him, or David? He was too saintly for this world, your cousin, Gilbert, and he would have given this estate all away if saner and wiser counsel had not prevailed with him.'

'Your counsel?' Nimue thought cynically, watching her. She was beginning to suspect that Dorabella's frequent visits to Grannah in the past to sit and sing to the lonely old man in the twilight had been calculated affairs, rather than the innocent devotion of a girl scarcely out of childhood. Recalling Jonas Mowas's round, florid face and ingenuous look, she spared the widower who found it difficult to cope with his wayward daughter a fleeting stab of sympathy.

'That old reprobate Pendragon was as bad,' Dorabella added suddenly, and Nimue felt her heart stir and bring her breath quickly to her throat. Mary, relieved that the conversation appeared to be progressing at last along lines she could comprehend, looked up from where she had just pricked her finger with her embroidery needle and was bleeding little drops of blood onto the tangled silks of her work.

'The wizard? I told Nimue of him and she said she had seen him, but it could not have been. He must be in his grave by now.'

Dorabella turned a glance of pale appraisal towards Nimue, and the young woman returned it steadily.

'Pendragon passed away some years ago,' she said. 'At least, it was generally assumed that he died in the manner of all flesh, though there were rumours that he had been carried off by demons. He had a son,' she added after a moment in her flat voice, unaware that she was bringing vivid enlightenment to Nimue, who realised now where the man from the sea had learned the names of the spirits, where his seemingly magical power to charm had been obtained. 'He is a hermit, all but, and does not mingle with society, though I know of many a girl who would risk her soul for his black hair and the strength of his shoulders. He has lived alone since his father died. There are rumours that he is league with the devil, and maybe he is. How else would he have escaped the fire that should have killed him?'

'Fire?' Nimue breathed, every nerve in her body suddenly alert so that she seemed to be quivering like an image seen through water – or through fierce heat. A vision of the crashing timbers and roaring flames came to her again, so that the room around her seemed to waver and darken, and the figure of Dorabella was very far away. The other young woman shrugged.

'That was how old Pendragon died. The tower caught fire one night, and Merlin Pendragon was trapped in the flames trying to save his father. The roof fell in, they say, and he was burned.' She turned to Nimue, her voice still light and cool. 'And you have seen him? Has he two eyes, or only one now? The blazing timbers burned his face and they say it took an eye.'

Nimue's heart contracted with horror and shock as she tried to comprehend what Dorabella had said. Compassion swept through her like a hot, searing dark flood, and comprehension too. So that was the secret of the vision. She had passed backwards in time, and not into the future. The fire, and its terrible aftermath, had already happened, the ashes had long since cooled, and been dispersed in the wind.

It seemed to her suddenly as though this was something she had always known, as though she had been present there that night when the desperate figure of the man tried to fight his way through the flames to the chamber where the old wizard slept. She saw again the falling timber, the heated furnaces of white ash, with clouds of red sparks bursting as the night wind caught them. Her own mournful cry, desolate as a lost and far-off bird calling, lamented through her brain once again and she felt as though she must have spoken the words aloud.

'My love, my love, my love.'

But no-one else had heard, no-one else had seen, and she managed to turn to Dorabella seemingly outwardly quite composed.

'I could not see his face clearly, but I am sure he had both his eyes. I saw them gleaming.'

Never should anyone know that she had shared the terror of that night, whether in her nightmares or by the strange power of love that can cut through time and place. Never should anyone be aware of the fateful bond that drew her to this man who hid his face in darkness. She felt as she had felt when they had spoken at Pendragon, weak at his very presence, her body shaken and trembling. But now she recognised the feeling for what it was, a sensation of tenderness so fierce it was like a sword in her heart. She must protect him, she must save him, though from what, she could not tell.

'His family, at any rate, is of noble lineage,' Dorabella said grudgingly. 'No house in a night for them. They have lived in that tower for generations, there have been Pendragons here since the days of Arthur.'

'Who - ?' Nimue began, then controlling her voice, she continued firmly: 'Who was his mother?'

'Old Pendragon never married. No women live there,' Dorabella stated with little interest. 'He might have been born of some water-sprite or dryad, who knows? But he was named the old man's heir, legally, my father says. Well, he is welcome to that crumbling ancient tower, no-one else would live there for sure, and the land is poor and of no use, it is just rock and scrub.'

An image came into Nimue's mind as she spoke. The young woman seemed to see, overlaid upon the room around her, Mary's satin skirts and fair curls, Gilbert's intent gaze upon Dorabella, and the other woman's fingers playing in a calculating manner with her rosary beads, a dark cavern beneath the ground, and the tiny flicker, she thought of a candle or a lantern.

Water dripped somewhere, and the wet stones gleamed. She could feel the pressure of the earth, the stillness of it all around her, and she knew suddenly that she must remember this. It was of immense import. A sensation of urgency possessed her, so that she could hardly keep her instincts in check. Somehow, in some way, she must go to Pendragon and tell him what she had seen.

But there was a right time for everything, her father had taught her, and as the days passed and the work of the household claimed her, the weather closing down on Grannah in driving mists of silver rain that cut them off from the rest of the world as effectively as if they had been marooned upon the top of mighty Snowdon itself, Nimue kept her counsel and watched for her time to return to Pendragon. The season turned, so that the festival of Samhain was upon them.

Her father, who had been, as he described it, 'As good a Catholic as any thinking man has any business to be,' had celebrated whatever festivals were to hand at any time of the year indiscriminately, and he taught Nimue to use whatever means presented themselves to communicate humbly and in thankfulness and joy for the abundance of living to 'The power at the end of the world, whatever or whoever it might be.'

Consequently, sometimes Gereint had worshipped in the Christian manner, and the household prayed to the saints at All Hallows and All Souls. In other years however, he had more pronouncedly favoured the 'old religion' and invoked the Celtic old hag, actively communicating with the world beyond as October drew to a close and the Celtic New Year dawned, taking the world into the dark month, November, and the dark night of the year.

On these October nights since coming to Grannah, Nimue had felt herself very close to the world of the spirits, her father and the restless dead who pressed themselves against the casement of her chamber, drawn to the light from the mysterious countryside about her. She had felt her powers, those powers of which her father had spoken – the powers which Pendragon himself had attributed to her – stirring within her so that she was merely a way, a channel for the force of a greater power than herself, submitting herself humbly to it. She

68

felt she was beginning to understand now how great and yet awesome was the legacy Gereint Gwynne had left her, her inheritance as a wise child, what it truly meant to be her father's daughter.

She sat on her window seat on the first night of the Dark Moon with the fur comforter wrapped close around her to guard against the chills of dank autumn, her hands stilled in her lap, the moonstone weighing heavy on her finger, her thoughts emptied, waiting, though she did not know what she was waiting for. Beyond the casement was the black night, and beyond that the deeper darkness she could not penetrate. She waited for enlightenment to come, knowing somehow that it would not fail her.

She felt the presence of her father very close, and was comforted. And then she felt herself wondering about her mother, the girl who had given her life even as she herself slipped away to the realms beyond, and whom she had never seen. Would her mother come to her to advise her on this most awful of nights? Would she hear a sweet, bell-like voice in the wind, giving her reassurance and courage?

But the wind held no voices, it blew empty and mournful and into her mind instead, as she sat waiting in the dark, came the image of the cavern she had seen when Dorabella Mowas had spoken of old Pendragon and his son, deep beneath the ground with the tiny melodious dripping of water, the gleam of dark glistening rock in the light of a wavering candle flame. And before she knew it, there had been a voice, it had come and it had spoken to her, though she had no recollection of hearing it.

' – Surely there is a vein for the silver, and a place for the gold where they fine it. Iron is taken out of the earth, and brass is molten out of the stone….As for the earth, out of it cometh bread: and under it is turned up as it were with fire. The stones of it are the place of sapphires; and it hath dust of gold….He putteth forth his hand upon the rock….his eye seeth every precious thing….the thing that is hid bringeth he forth to light….But where shall wisdom be found? And where is the place of understanding?'

Nimue had pondered for a long time afterwards on these words, which had impressed themselves on her mind as though the voice had written them there in letters of fire, but she had no idea of their meaning. She had turned them over and over, trying to read their message. But it had not been for her, she knew. It was for Pendragon, and he alone would understand it.

And now the time had come, and in the gathering dusk, she and Llew made their way along the rough roads from Flint and the comfortable cosiness of Ignatius Smith's house, beeswaxed by Emma and the maids, with the promise of a visit to teach Mistress Mary the secrets of Welshcakes – and a meaningful declaration from the lawyer that he would deem it a pleasure to accompany his sister. Nimue found herself peering ahead into the gloom as though the light of the candle that flickered in the window of Pendragon tower was a beacon that flared in the darkness, its light illuminating all with gold.

And yet, she knew within her that it was not the tower that drew her but the man himself. It was Merlin Pendragon, faery-born, who had passed through the flames to emerge tempered as steel, who was the beacon to light up her life and guide her days, he who was the fire at which her spirit might warm itself and know that it was safely home. Her heart was beating fast as the tower came into view, lowering through the trees, and she slid from her pony and bade Llew wait for her with the beasts, and ran up the stony dark path to the door and knocked upon it fiercely with her riding crop.

6

His eyes were not gleaming now, they were ablaze with dark fire. For some reason to which Nimue was not privy, he seemed in a state of tightly controlled rage. His tall, solid outline blocked the narrow doorway where a welcoming gleam of light, whether fire or candle, she could not tell, glowed beyond, and he leaned forward, peering over her shoulder into the dimness of the avenue of trees, deliberately turning his head from her as she stood irresolute before him.

When he spoke, his voice was low, but there was some fierce undercurrent beneath the surface of his words that caused her heart to beat faster with alarm. Had she made a grave mistake in coming here? What, after all, did she really know about this man? In the dimness, feeling tension almost palpable on the air, she thought with sudden fright that perhaps the gossips were right. Perhaps he too was in league with the devil, carrying on the tradition of his father, the wizard.

'Ah, so it is the witch, and she comes when she chooses, expecting a welcome. And your groom, mistress, where is he? For you have not walked the miles to me through this dark afternoon. You have left him to cool his heels in the forest, no doubt, along with your beasts.' As she stared, he added brusquely: 'Wait and I will tell Huw to bring him in, and see to the ponies.'

Nimue found her fears abating at the very triviality of his words. Her sense of expectation and urgency dwindled to nothing. But what had she expected, she thought, biting her lip in absurd disappointment that this bright dream, like all dreams, seemed to be fast fading in the bleak light of reality. Suddenly conscious of her surroundings, the wet and the melancholy of the day, she shivered, trying to resist a dismaying urge to dissolve into foolish, womanly tears.

She took a deep breath and drew herself erect, wrapping her pride around her and attempting to speak coolly. She felt sorry that she had come.

'Indeed, there is no necessity, sir.'

But her words and her movement of withdrawal only seemed to enflame him further. He reached out with a long arm and seized the hand that was tightening her cloak close about her throat, saying as he pulled her stumbling after him across the threshold: 'Oh, is there not, indeed? And if he is not carried off by a wraith woman for his bright eyes, I suppose you will not care that you lose him and your beasts to the weather? Are you not aware that it will be a hard frost tonight, witch, a killing frost?'

Nimue could not see his face but she was only too conscious of the hands that were propelling her roughly into a dimly lit cavern of a chamber. Involuntarily, blinded and disorientated, she let out a loud gasp of fright and he let her go immediately, so that she had to reel dazedly on her feet in an effort to regain her balance.

She was utterly at a loss as to why this intimidating heir to a kingdom of spirits so obviously felt the need to shout her down before she had so much as spoken a word. It was inexplicable. Why, the last time they had met, he had not only seemed reasonably pleased to see her, but had presented her (though she had to admit, just as inexplicably), with the moonstone.

'A killing frost – tonight?' she repeated helplessly, her fears once more ebbing in exasperation at the very irrelevance of his words.

'Tonight,' he assured her ominously, breathing hard. He added in a rather more controlled, but still derisive tone: 'But I can see you could keep from me no longer and must come all unbidden and with no warning whatever the state of the weather, in your eagerness to spend this night with me.'

Her mouth opened like a little bird's, but this time she could not utter so much as a squeak. She stood breathless, gaping at him, while he crashed shut the heavy door, seeming to give this performance far more attention than was necessary. She was rubbing the wrist which ached from his grip and was trying to frame words that would extricate her from this increasingly ridiculous situation when he turned, laid a hand on her shoulder and pushed her unceremoniously through an archway and a deeply shadowed vault of a hall, and into a further chamber. It was so quickly done that she had no chance to protest.

The first thing she was aware of was that the chamber was unexpectedly warm and bright with the soft light of candles. When she had gathered her wits together for a few moments, sitting on the black high-backed oak chair to which he had propelled her, thrusting her down with a twist of a wrist like iron, she was able to see, reassuringly, that her surroundings were more than comfortable. They were gracious, surprisingly spacious and with a low carved ceiling above. The walls were of roughly hewn stone over which were hung tapestries of great beauty, though their colours were dimmed with years.

In the centre of the room stood an object Nimue had never thought to see in this remote country to which she had come, though on reflection, she supposed it might have been natural enough for a wizard to have possessed such a thing in his house. It was made of black wood, a great globe of the heavens, inlaid with mother-of-pearl. Looking about her, intrigued now, she could see too that there were charts and compasses and all the instruments for working with the planets and the stars, outspread upon a wide table.

At the sight of the globe and the charts, Nimue felt an overwhelming awareness of destiny, of fatefulness within her. She seemed to have reached the end of a long journey. At last, guided by an unseen hand, she had come home. At any moment she would see her father's fingers touch the starry globe, as he had touched his own similar one in the little room in London, and hear his voice naming the planets as he noted their positions in the astrological houses, marking them with his quill. She sat unable to move, while memories and impressions whirled in the air about her and she was too overcome to speak.

There was a silver jug standing on a chest, and Pendragon lifted it and poured out wine into a tarnished goblet with a soft silvery sheen. He held it out to her, and Nimue took it without a word and drank. The wine was sweet, and tasted of flowers. It warmed her so much, filling her veins with a sensation of golden light, that after a moment she was able to address the man who stood regarding her, even though the could not see him clearly, his lean body seeming to drift in and out of the focus of her eyes.

She wondered briefly, in a distant corner of her mind, whether he had imprisoned her under some sort of spell, for the words she wanted to utter, of wonder at the globe of the heavens, of the surfacing of dear, but searingly painful memories of her father, did not materialise. Instead she found herself saying, in the most brazen and familiar of tones:

'You are impertinent, sir, yes and more than impertinent. How do you know that I will not report your behaviour to Gilbert – I mean, to Mister Stoneyathe, and that he will not send the sheriff to arrest you.'

'Oh, and what is my crime? Giving shelter to a lost and weary traveller?' he retorted, turning to the table, his hands busy with the parchments. His voice, as well as his dark figure, was not easy to identify clearly. Nimue found it was fading in and out of her hearing in an exceedingly strange manner, much to her discomfiture.

'Not to mention the trouble I have gone to in order to care for your groom and your beasts,' he went on, turning back to stare at her, and folding his arms across his chest. 'You are, I am sorry indeed to say it, but I must speak the truth, witch, in no fit state whatever to travel. Or at least,' he added, in a tone which sounded off a loud alarm in her head, 'you will be in no fit state to travel when that wine you are drinking has done its work.'

She was suddenly dry-mouthed, in spite of the sweet flowery taste of the liquid.

'Ah, so you would refuse my hospitality, would you, witch? What is this excess of pure and virginal virtue?'

She should have been trembling, pleading with him, but beneath the floating of her brain, Nimue was conscious that he spoke like an actor, playing a part. Although, she could not understand why he should pronounce his words so forcefully, in a voice that was much too loud. It was as though he did not dare to stop speaking – or even allow her to say anything – in case he revealed something else, something she was not meant to know. And then enlightenment came. But surely not! Surely, she thought unbelievingly, surely the mighty Pendragon, lord of the tower, and with legions of teeming airy spirits at his call, could not actually be *afraid*? And – of her?

'God's blood, woman,' he proclaimed, ringing out the oath in a manner that Will Shakespeare might have envied. 'Do you believe I will ravish you? Ha, what else am I expected to do, by Azrael? Do you not continually hound and pester me beyond endurance, even at my very door?' He took breath before continuing in the manner of one grievously wronged, and as though she might interrupt him, though her senses by now were quivering with incredulous laughter, and she could not have framed a single word.

'With the help of Jesu and the saints I do abjure temptation. Heaven forfend!' Pendragon declared piously, crossing himself. 'You shall have a virginal bed for the night, and in the morning I will personally conduct you home to Grannah.'

This final – and disappointing – blow to her expectations was too much for Nimue, and when she looked up she saw that his face was alight with a kind of gleeful triumph, as though he had bested her at wrestling, or cards. Her discomfiture was complete. She sat foolishly in her chair, not knowing what to answer him, but at the sight of her dismay, his black eyes lost their triumph and their fire. His voice came hoarsely.

'Let it be, I will not see you thus, your head bowed and you helpless, witch. For in spite of me, I am fired with such rage as to who has done this to you that I must kill him, and yet it is myself with my clumsy words, and I cannot kill myself.' He paused for a moment, then spoke in a different tone. Nimue felt as though she was hearing his true voice for the first time, husky and deep, yet now strangely hesitant, as though he was groping in areas foreign to him.

'Of your charity, forgive a wretch who has lived for too long away from the company of fair women,' he said.

But it was not only his voice which held her now so that she was transfixed, unable to move, staring up at him as he put out his hand in a wry gesture of mock-surrender. The childish game had indeed changed into a confrontation that was fierce and deep. There was pain here, as well as passion. Her breath caught in her throat and hot tears started to her eyes, born of confusion and weariness and the potency of the wine. But born too of an almost unbearable anguish that seemed to pierce her through the heart for he did not turn from her, and she saw his face fully in the light of the candles.

'Your face,' she whispered, stricken, lifting her clenched fist to her mouth. 'Oh, your face.'

He was very still, and then his hand moved to the great twisted scar that ran down from the thick black hair to the strong line of his jaw. He half-turned instinctively from her.

'The mark of the fire. I had forgotten that I must terrify you,' he said quietly. The awkward buffoon had vanished at last, and she recognised him now. The colours of the dream were back, shimmering around her, transforming the chamber, and reflecting from his eyes.

'No, oh no,' she cried, sobbing in real earnest and hardly aware of what was the reality and what was the vision, or what that other terrible dream. 'Oh, never, never. I saw the fire, I was there, it was I who called to you then and I could not save you. Oh, I could not save you, and so you were burned, my - .' Then suddenly she tried to check herself, confused and distressed but the low whisper came from her lips despite herself. 'My – love.'

It seemed as though the word crystallised into form between them, an expression of the truth of their meeting with all else stripped from it, a gift of purity and passion, clear as ice, beautiful as crystal. It hung there for a moment, trembling, then he said slowly, as though he was dazed and just awaking from a deep sleep:

'And now, tell me why you came here tonight.'

The warmth of the room as well as the wine was spreading through her, and she was as light-headed and as giddy as she had been before when she had been near him. It was inexplicable. Nimue had always prided herself on her self-possession, but now she felt as though she stood outside herself, while her body burned, in thrall to him. The turbulent emotions of the past weeks seemed to crowd in upon her, overlaid by the strangeness and inevitability of the moment. She recalled, as though she lived through them again in the blink of an eye, the forced journey into a new life, a new future – and then her pleasure at Will's visit, the subtle reaching out from her past life in London and all the stirred up emotions, difficult to identify, but which she knew she could not take from her old friend and seemingly must let go for ever. There had been a loss, a mourning, and in and out of it all was woven the wavering of the hopes that had flowered and the dreams she had dreamed at the window of her chamber at Grannah, the visions and echoes of her father's words.

' – in the west, it must be Stoneyathe – you will discover who you really are – and find your true love and the desire of your heart for ever - .'

And now he was here, and he was not Gilbert Stoneyathe, nor Will with his silver tongue and his town manners, but this diffident, impossible yet utterly compelling man who had begun to haunt her as soon as she had seen him. He was here before her in the light, where the scars on his face were clearly visible, etched by the candles' luminosity, and his eyes were on her, intent and forceful, no pretence now but the truth, and the truth left her weak and helpless.

Nimue gave a long sigh, releasing all the pent-up tensions within her. This was the tide on which she must be borne along, the sea in which she must drown, the way in which it had to be. She leaned gratefully against the wooden back of her chair, and took the goblet which he had refilled, lifting it to her mouth while she watched him over the rim. She had lost herself in the awkwardness of their meeting, and he too had been unsure, but she had found herself now.

'You know why I came,' she said at length, and he nodded, asking no questions. He had found himself also and he spoke softly, without artifice.

'Yes. Yet there is a darkness, an emptiness you carry with you, not your own. You have brought it for me, witch, for me to fill, I think.'

He spoke the truth, she thought, dazzled. He would fill every corner, light all her dark places. For ever and ever. But then, as he waited, watching her, she tried to recall the more pressing realities, that other reason for her visit to Pendragon tower.

'There is word for you, a message,' she began, wondering how best to explain the vision to him. 'I have the sight, I have seen it – and also heard the words. There was a dark cave, somewhere beneath the earth, with the tiny dripping of water. I saw rocks gleaming black, and a lantern flame, and heard the hush of the silence. And when I sat alone on the night of the Dark Moon, I heard the words, impressing themselves upon my mind and I saw the cave again, the same vision as before.'

'A dark cave somewhere beneath the earth?' he repeated.

'Yes. I cannot tell you where, save that it is of importance to you. It may even,' she added, with sudden intuitive clarity, 'be a matter of your life or death. And there were the words.'

'The words? What words?' he asked, and she repeated them, lingering over their richness and power.

' – a vein for the silver and a place for the gold…a place of sapphires; and it hath dust of gold…every precious thing…the thing that is hid bringeth he forth to light…But where shall wisdom be found? And where is the place of understanding?'

Pendragon's voice was hushed, like a sigh, in the pause after Nimue had finished speaking.

'Those are my father's words. This was his legacy to me. He tried to tell me – on the night of the fire - .'

She was silent, overcome with awe at the wonder of it, content to sit, to wait for him to enlighten her. She thought she could sit for ever, out of time, in this quiet chamber where the tapestries quivered in rich life on the walls and the heavens were outspread before her so that she could reach out her fingers and touch the stars. But there was a movement at the chamber door and a slight figure in a white robe entered, and stood quietly with folded arms and hands hidden in long, all-concealing sleeves. The man's face was old and the skin dark, almost black, but the soft halo round the gnarled features was pale as snow, and the eyes, Nimue saw, unable to stop herself staring in fascination, were pale also, almost white, unlike any eyes she had ever seen. Lines creased the age-worn countenance, giving it the texture of a walnut, richly glowing. Pendragon spoke in the Welsh tongue, and the old man moved his head in assent with the greatest dignity, then silently withdrew.

'Huw,' Pendragon explained, seeing Nimue's gaze lingering on the closed door. 'My manservant. He is dumb.'

'Huw? He is then Welsh? I cannot think so, I have seen men of his dark race as freaks in London,' Nimue could not help saying, and Pendragon gazed sombrely into the candle flame.

'He was the only living soul to survive a wreck upon these shores sixty years ago, my father took him in and nursed him back to health. He was but a boy then, and God knows what he was doing on that vessel, or the life intended for him. He is a *castrato*, neither man nor woman, and his tongue had been cut out. My father never knew if he had a name.' He added in a lighter tone: 'So he suffered the baptism of an honest Christian in our northern seas, and survived it to become Huw. Huw he will always be. Welsh is the only language he knows, and as he served my father, so he serves me. He will serve you too,' he told Nimue. 'He is skilled in the magic of his race and what my father taught him.'

'Dorabella Mowas says you are in league with the devil,' Nimue found herself saying, the wine loosening her tongue, and to her discomfiture he replied calmly:

'Perhaps I am.'

She roused herself. 'No, I would never believe that of you for a moment.'

'Others do,' he said mildly.

'They do not know you,' Nimue declared, and his eyes challenged her.

'And you know me so well then?'

'I know - ,' she began, then stopped and put down her goblet. 'I know – what I know.'

He regarded her thoughtfully for a long moment, then asked:

'The vision, the cave. That is all? You can tell me no more?'

'No more. But that I knew I must come to you. I thought,' she said simply, 'that you would know what it meant.'

He did not answer. He paced the width of the chamber, touched one of the compasses on the table, frowning down at it. His body was as easy as a cat, for all its length, taut and controlled. Nimue found that her gaze lingered on his back with a sensation of intense pleasure, drinking in the planes of his bones beneath the rough jerkin. In fascination, her gaze fell lower to the play of muscle in his lean thighs, above the worn leather of his boots. She flushed as he turned, considering her.

'Will you go, or stay? I will not detain you against your will, though there is indeed a bed in the tower for you, with my mother's quilt, that she worked in patches of silks and velvets in the months she waited for my birth. You already have her ring. And her blessing. And your groom can sleep in the stable, he will not freeze there.'

'How did you know I would come?' Nimue could not help asking, and he smiled down at her slowly for the first time since she had glimpsed his dark form in the waves, his white horse waiting.

'I did not know. But I was content to wait. And here you are.'

He reached out with his right hand, and as though a magnet drew her, she lifted hers and took it, feeling as she did so that she was sealing a pact already long agreed. His fingers closed round hers, hard and warm, but there was a roughness upon them against her skin, and she turned his hand to the light to look. It was scarred like his face, puckering half into whiteness.

'The fire,' she breathed, as though another blow went home to her heart.

'Yes. But that is all,' he said steadily, his voice compelling her. 'There are no more scars for you to find.'

She looked up at him then, gazing into the shifting colours of his eyes, and was seized by a sudden memory, a recollection gone even before she had grasped it. But surely she had looked into those same eyes before, in a distant time, known that same face, and felt the touch of that same hand. She drew a breath to speak, but even as she began to form the words, the image had slipped away and when or how, she could not remember.

'I think – I have always known you,' she whispered, hardly aware of what she said. 'I had you and then I lost you. I think I have always loved you, but we were parted. It was the fire that took you from me. I thought I would never find you again.'

'I am here, as you are,' he told her softly, and for a moment it was as though they were apart and the world did not exist, only their two selves, frozen into an eternal exchange of passion that had no need to be spoken. 'Will you leave me once again alone in this life? Or will you brave the tower and my mother's quilt?'

She would have promised him anything in that moment, but into her consciousness through the far wild distances of the evening came the note of a bell, and she lifted her head, recalled to reality.

'What is that sound?'

'Sometimes if the wind is fair, I hear the bell they still ring at the abbey at Basingwerk,' he told her, adding quietly, as he watched her face: 'My father is buried nearby.'

Nimue turned to look at the globe of the heavens.

'Your father – the wizard?' she asked. 'And you? Are you a wizard also?'

'I was born on the natal day of Our Lord,' Pendragon told her easily. 'Mercury on the ascendant, Saturn on the descendant.'

'Light and dark,' Nimue said, involuntarily.

'And you? No, I will tell you. Venus in Libra, for sure, for your beauty. And Jupiter also. We will draw up the charts and compare them. The moon eclipsed on our south nodes, that was where we met and parted in another life.'

Nimue drew in her breath in delight, but once more she heard the far-flung note of the bell, summoning her back into the world where Gilbert and his sister were awaiting her return, where Morfydd and the maids were flushed and busy in the kitchen, and where Ignatius Smith and Mistress Emma would be calling in a week to impart the secret of Welshcakes. She hesitated, troubled.

'I am stayed for at Grannah,' she said, uncertainly, but he only smiled again, easily.

'One day, I will light the candles in the tower.'

Nimue took heart at his understanding. She did not need to explain, he was aware of her sudden hesitation, her fear. He knew her better than she knew herself.

'I will come again,' she said, unwilling to leave him now that she knew he would let her go.

'Tomorrow?' He was laughing at her openly, his dark eyes burning with dangerous fire.

She lifted her head. 'If you need me.'

'And if you need me, come,' he told her, the laughter suddenly gone. Then as though he feared what further words might pass his lips, he set them firmly together, saying no more.

Nimue drank in the candle-lit mask of light and shadow that was his face. She no longer saw the scars, only the strength and nobility of his high-boned cheeks and forehead, the straight nose and the curve of his mouth, bespeaking passion as well as restraint and command. She thought she could read that face for eternity and never tire of it.

But as she gazed, fascinated, he turned to light her to the door, once more tall and aloof, and then she found she was standing in the vaulted hall pulling her cloak round her while the white-robed Huw silently opened the great door. The wind blew in out of the darkness, rattling the tapestries in the room behind her, trailing the candle flames into uncertain streamers of light. She saw the outline of Llew's thin dark shadow with her pony and as though in a dream, her limbs moving without volition, she went forward to mount it from the water trough, trying to remember that there were other worlds yet outside Pendragon and its spell, the spell of the man and his chamber where peace lay upon the charts and the silvery globe of the heavens.

For her own sake, lest she lose herself, she must gather herself together, regain her poise, her independence of spirit. She had disdained to be a servant to Gilbert, so why then should the thought of laying her heart and soul at Merlin Pendragon's feet seem like the next best thing to heaven? She heard him laughing, softly, as she rode off into the trees.

7

By the time the household at Grannah had retired and she was alone with her thoughts, curled up warmly within the depths of her bed, but with sleep far from her, Nimue was seething with frustration. To have seen him, to have spoken to him, and yet to have said so little. She had meant to tell him so many things. She wanted to know everything about him, and to tell him everything about herself – how had it happened then that she had come away filled with silence between them, all her words and her questions unspoken?

Her mind turned to Pendragon's father, that strange and mysteriously powerful figure, the old wizard, who lay now within the sound of the lonely bell at Basingwerk Abbey. So he had indeed died, despite all tales to the contrary, in the manner of all flesh, and had been laid to rest by his son with as much reverence as any other dearly esteemed parent. Nimue bit her lip at the thought. She wanted suddenly to tell Pendragon about her own father, of what his loss had meant to her. She wanted to be able to weep for Gereint Gwynne in Pendragon's arms.

And she wanted to know more of Pendragon's mother, that elusive faery creature who had seemingly been human enough to work a quilt of silks and velvets while she dreamed the long months away in the tower, awaiting the birth of her child. She of the moonstone ring that Nimue wore on her own finger now, heavy with the power that dragged the tides and the months in their appointed courses, and yet translucent with the colours of nothing.

But at the thought of the tower, all drowsiness fled. Nimue wanted more than anything to see the tower. And its room, that promised room where the fateful quilt lay spread and the candles were waiting – for herself. She felt her cheeks burn in the darkness as the hot blood beat up in her face, and she turned her head into the cool linen of her pillow.

Oh, did he think her a wanton, as the rest of the world surely would if they knew how she had so nearly forced her way into his bed? Little wonder, she thought with a smothered gulp of laughter bubbling in her throat at the recollection of his discomfiture, he had declared himself tempted to ravish her.

But hard on the heels of this thought came another. He had been tempted, he had admitted it himself, but though she would of course have been horrified if he had attempted to force his will upon her, horrified, hurt and disenchanted, yet – he had not even tried. He had done nothing. He had laughed, and let her go. A quiver chilled the cheeks from which the surge of hot blood had in as many minutes suddenly drained. Did he not – it was an unthinkable prospect, but – could it have been that he did not find her desirable?

But even as fingers of panic began to flutter her heart, her inner vision focussed on the image of that face, so terribly scarred, bent to hers, and she knew beyond any foolish doubts that when the time came, she would go to him in the certainty that he would be waiting for her. There was no need to fear for his steadfastness, or attempt to play the coquette. It had all been settled long ago, when their moons had eclipsed on the south nodes. He had said that himself too.

Nimue burrowed more deeply into the comfort of her feather mattress – for cousin David had considered such items not as luxury but a healthy necessity on the best beds in his house, rather than the customary straw pallet. She pulled the coverlet and heavy fur comforter softer against her chin so that only the top of her head poked up into the chill darkness of the chamber. She luxuriated in the warmth, smiling secretly in the dark, hugging herself. She did not dare to anticipate what that lean body would feel like against hers. But when she drifted into sleep, it was to dream of Pendragon's arms surrounding her, his hands, those long, strong hands whose touch she already knew, gathering her close against his heart.

Winters at Grannah were wild and iron-hard, and when Nimue might have been laughing in the torchlight of frosty London streets, in company with Will Shakespeare and his player companions, as she had done so many times with her father, eating hot chestnuts and drinking mulled ale wherever crowds gathered, she now saw how snow fell heavily on the hills, making ways too deep for the ponies, and heard the mourning of the wind from the far mountains in the west. The killings of *Tachwedd*, ready for the cold season, were long done, and the house must be kept warm with fires for the master and his sister, and as a haven for the men and maids whose daily duties took them into the teeth of the weather, to return half-frozen, with red noses and pinched hands, raw with icicles.

The beasts must be seen to whatever the weather and the necessities of the household fetched. Food was constantly simmering or on the spit over the cavernous fire in the kitchen and there were the regular days of baking, brewing, and preparations not only for the demands of the household but for the festivities that would mark the Christmas festival and the turn of the year.

Morfydd and the maids described to Nimue how Gilbert's cousin David had kept Christmas with open house, in the tradition of all great estates – for David, whatever his actual status, had obviously, she thought, possessed the instincts of a gentleman, a true aristocrat. Travellers were welcome one and all, and there was punch and frumenty enough for everyone, as well as stale beer and slabs of cold meat. Even the most pinched and ragged of the poor 'walking Welsh' were given stout fare if they ventured into the yard at Grannah at the Christmas season, and there were many in small cottages and even farms on the estate who had blessed the master of Grannah as a saint.

Cousin David, it seemed, had not held with parsons, nor even with popery, either, though the old traditions of Catholicism flourished strongly in many parts of Wales. But unlike the wizard, who, as Nimue recollected from Jonas Mowas' spirited account, had followed the 'old religion', cousin David did not seem to have practised any formal religion at all, and had apparently never set foot in a church for years, though he had been buried in all solemnity, with the Bishop himself conducting the funeral service, in St Asaph, in the monument of his forbears.

When Gilbert heard about the monument, he had vowed to himself that he would build a far more splendid one for his own dynasty and authorised Ignatius Smith to enter into negotiations with the church at Caerwys, in the belief that he would achieve more by being the patron of a smaller church, than one of the many patrons of a cathedral. He considered whatever he spent in securing his future in posterity in a monument of marble, money well invested.

But he was becoming grudging in parting with his money for the sake of charity, and at first it seemed unlikely that he would enter wholeheartedly into the spirit of the Christmas season, for the idea of the Welsh poor setting so much as a foot on his estates and the land he now regarded as his, fenced for the pasture of more and more of the sheep who would spin their wool into gold for him, had become anathema. But, realising that he would forfeit the goodwill of his neighbours, local gentry and farmers, of the likes of Jonas Mowas, he contented himself with setting mantraps in the woods and employing a new bailiff to patrol his hastily erected fences.

Further to curry the favour of society, he gave employment to several more local lads and girls, though his motive was pride, for he told Nimue he would have Grannah a mansion fit for the Queen herself to visit. A place of refinement and culture. This expense too was worth the reputation he hoped to build up for himself among those who effectively ruled this part of

Flintshire. For it would be one of their daughters who would marry his son, his heir, and graft his name onto the stock of the county. His second son might marry among the Cheshire gentry. And Gilbert was already speculating on the usefulness of daughters in the marriage market. When Dorabella was present, he would sit regarding her fixedly, while his mind formulated its plans, and Mary lost herself in schemes of entrapping Mister Smith.

Nimue turned housewife with a newly light heart, conscious of her duties as the nominal mistress of Grannah – until such a time as Dorabella or some other woman should oust her, she was well aware but by then, who knew, she might be the lady of a higher and wilder tower. Meantime, prudence counselled that she must not forget she owed her welfare, her bed and board to Gilbert and his sister. For in spite of the magic that had lit her visit to Pendragon tower, she was still a romantic fool enough to want words from the lips of the man to whom she would willingly give all, reassuring her that he would not ask her for such a sacrifice. She would wait until he offered her formally those treasures beyond price, his name, his heart and his hand.

But as she rose and lit her candle in the snowy dark of the December mornings, and broke the ice on the pails, her breath a cloud as she crossed the yard, Nimue repeated words to herself, hugging them to her as though they would warm her through. Morfydd and Llew and the rest were teaching her the Welsh tongue, and being Celts, to whom music was their first language, they taught her by means of music and song.

'I sing of my warrior, my prince,
Tall among the heroes, strong
As the force of thunder,
His tongue silver as lightning,
Piercing me like an arrow.'

That was what the words meant, Morfydd had told her, and in these ice-laden white-dark mornings, it seemed to Nimue perfectly natural that she should sing of love, and of him. And though unaware of Nimue's feeling for Pendragon, Morfydd's dark eyes like bright berries sparkled, her plump cheeks were ruddy as she held the tune for Nimue in her rich contralto. The Welsh loved love ballads, they loved lovers, and many were the songs written by some of the princes themselves, she told Nimue, in praise of their beautiful women.

Morfydd had lost her man at sea, and had been rescued from the grinding hopelessness of dismal poverty by cousin David, who had given her a place at Grannah, where she could keep herself and Llew. And now Grannah was their home, the household could not do without her, and the memory of the dark lad with the laughing eyes had been replaced by the more sober features of one of the drovers who wanted to marry her in the spring.

Gilbert secretly counted himself fortunate that he could leave the house to Nimue's increasingly capable ministrations, and now that he had the new bailiff and a small army of new labour to see to the work of the estate, he had revived his former ambition and addressed himself to escorting Mary to as many fashionable halls and parlours as he could procure invitations and entrée. Mary, who shivered at a draught and complained at the slightest inconvenience nevertheless regarded half a day's journey on horseback – almost lost in the drifts and with chattering teeth within her heavy velvet hood and cloak, the sheepskin old Sion threw round her shoulders evil-smelling – as but a small price to pay for the delight of society, for suppers with music, madrigals, laughter and convivial talk.

Nimue, watching with the springing joy of her own secret happiness, thought with repressed amusement that Mary had the stoicism of a hardened warrior of many campaigns, and a far greater endurance than anyone would have thought possible for such a feather-pate, and all for the sake of preening herself in her fine feathers in the company of equally feather-pated ladies who attended such frivolous pursuits, each one searching for prey of her own in the form of a husband.

In addition Mary had defied cousin David's edicts concerning hunting and had roused herself on several occasions to attend meets, clinging grimly onto her saddlebow even though her velvet caps and plumes had disappeared in pursuit of the chase and her blue satin skirts been ruined. She had been with Gilbert to the butts to watch the archers, and had seen Dorabella display an amazingly skilful aim with a bow. Positively an Amazon, as Gilbert had remarked in a manner that combined cold disapproval with a fascination that excited him beyond measure.

Nimue's sweet beauty had been noised abroad by Jonas Mowas whose heart, beneath his bluster, was as big as a barn door, and as a pensioner of the family, she had been invited, albeit somewhat vaguely, to accompany Gilbert and Mary on their excursions. She had been with them to Flint and Chester, to sit entranced amid the company as the board was cleared after supper and they turned to their music. Candlelight played over the dark high-boned Celtic faces, young Tudor and the cousin of Llwyd of Pentremeirchion, whose sister had married the son of the Earl of Ruthie, and become a Countess.

Nimue saw in the leaping flames and shadows, the image of that scarred face with its mouth of firmness and restraint which yet promised it would be unutterably tender when the moment came for tenderness. She could not help contrasting his solitude and strength with the flutterings and foolishness of the young men who clustered round her, much to Mary's suspicious annoyance. Though Nimue had found herself hard pressed to entrap the lawyer for Mary, she had not as yet allowed the other woman to pin her down to details of exactly what sort of spell she might perform – and indeed, had no intention of ever carrying out such activity – but when Mary saw how the men were drawn to Nimue's dark fragility, and the contrast of her blazing green-gold eyes, vivid with life, she immediately suspected magical intervention, assuming jealously that Nimue was trying to gain a husband first.

Nimue realised what the other woman was thinking, and was careful to keep herself apart from the merry flirtations, and dalliance that here in this wild country, was not by any means as courtly as she had been used to in London. She could not help men paying her their attention, but she could, and did, respond with a cool lack of enthusiasm. She reminded herself over and over that, as her father's daughter, she must step warily.

She thought constantly of Pendragon, wondering about him, the child who had grown to manhood in that lonely tower with a wizard for his father and the memory of a sweet presence haunting the room where her quilt still lay, for his mother. A man who walked alone, who followed his own path. Nimue longed to know everything there was to know about him. She thought of her father's amusement and what he would advise if he had been with her.

'What, the wizard's daughter spelled by the wizard's son? Dare all for love, Nimue, and its alchemy will transform this dross of a life to richness past comparing. I know. I dared all for your mother, and though she passed from me when you came into the world, yet we had touched the Blessed Isles and walked hand in hand along their shores. That was worth everything.'

On the eve of Christmas, Nimue had a dream. She seemed to be wandering on the hills above Pendragon, the snowy wastes spread dark-white below her. She was not touching the ground, but seemed to be floating, and all around her the sky was bitter with snow and the wind howled. Then, somewhere below, she saw a light, and felt it draw her. There was a lantern bobbing on the hillside, and a man was carrying it. He looked up as she neared him, and she saw that though he was unfamiliar to her, yet he knew her and had recognised her.

Once, Gereint Gwynne had shown Nimue a pack of cards which were old and rich, with strange pictures upon them. She recalled one of them as she looked into the face of the old man in her dream. It was the same, a figure in a rough robe and cowl, carrying a lantern from which light spilled, though there was a shutter on the lantern so that the light did not fall on the man's face and it remained dark.

He looked like a hermit, someone who lived far from the ways of men, and around him, crouched in the snow, were the figures of birds and small animals, like a painting she had seen in Arabella Nevile's missal at Court, of Saint Francis. There was peace and holiness around him that was visible as the snowy cloud of his breath, hanging on the air.

He spoke to Nimue in her dream, but she did not understand the words.

'*Dyma 'n awr. Ac aur. Awr.*'

Then he reached out a hand and lightly touched the top of her head in blessing. And then she was alone with only the wind, the words he had spoken tossed around her like falling stars.

The vision remained with her throughout the morning of Christmas Day, which Gilbert and Mary celebrated in the sort of style they were accustomed to in London. The mistletoe ball hung in the hall, and the white berries shone with the gleam of past mysteries. Gilbert had had the men bring in a Yule log from the forest and it burned majestically, while the feasting would begin later, when dinner was served to the master and the mistress and all at the hour of eleven.

Nimue had woken to the chill morning, black with ice and with a tiny silver crescent moon hanging on the end of the night, in the consciousness that this was Pendragon's natal day. She had not asked him the year of his birth, and longed to do so, in order that she could calculate his chart, although she thought she knew what she would find there, apart from what he had told her – his sun in Capricorn, Mercury on the ascendant, Saturn on the descendant. The signs of life and death, of suffering overcome, of warmth of heart and the humility of the truly great. Pendragon, whatever else he might be, was no child, no spoiled schemer like Gilbert, no fresh-faced youth nor worn ancient like the gentry she had met in the town houses of Chester, he was a man.

Nimue, going out for water early, cast a glance in the direction of the stars, and in the manner of all young women in love, wished upon them for the desire of her heart. What would it be? It was formless, for if Pendragon was only there, then all would be well. She thought she could ask for no more.

Cottagers from the neighbouring hamlets and farms, young men and old stalwarts came in a body wassailing and Gilbert, cold and aloof in his fine Court doublet, smiled with his lips only upon them as they toasted Grannah with smacking jokes English and Welsh, and the Wassail Bowl went round. The bells could be heard sounding from somewhere on the thin wintry air and Nimue, stopping for a moment in the bustle of the house, sent her thoughts with them to Pendragon tower, where she supposed he would be sitting alone in the quiet chamber with the globe of the heavens, waited on by the silent Huw.

But as it drew on to noon, she was surprised to discover that she had been mistaken. Not for Pendragon the ascetic lack of company and Spartan fare she had attributed to his tastes. For he came in person to Grannah and appeared in the yard riding his white horse, dark in the finest of velvet and slashed leather, sitting his mount like some ancient prince in his saddle, part of the beast. And not only that but he behaved with the manners of such a prince, giving his name with impressive *savoir faire* to the old man who asked his business and desiring in the most courteous of tones, to be announced to the master of the house.

Such civilised behaviour from one who for years had been regarded by the neighbourhood as a solitary recluse who possessed no social graces at all, and who was more accustomed to dealing with demons than his fellows – though the gossips might have been surprised if they had been aware of the true nature of Pendragon's activities, his reputation among scholars and learned men who had known his father, for instance – was enough to cause a sensation throughout Grannah. The maids, prudently crossing themselves against the evil eye, nevertheless turned to tiptoe and peer out of windows, mouths agape and breasts heaving beneath their bodices, as they calculated the breadth of Pendragon's shoulders and the tautness of his waist. The men sourly assured each other that his face was enough to frighten any wench away. But Morfydd, ever a realist, was heard to remark wistfully that there was a man worth the risking of a woman's immortal soul.

'All that is in the next world,' she commented practically. '*Duw*, but for those arms, and the way he sits his horse and the height of him to warm me in this world, I would be willing enough to trade whatever comes after.'

The household was at dinner, the merrymaking and feasting alike loosening the tongues and the polite formality of Mary and Mistress Emma Smith, who with her brother had been invited to Grannah for the festivities, so that they shrieked with laughter. Gilbert never lost his cool composure under any circumstances now, and he was talking business with Ignatius Smith, even though it was a day of festival.

There were signs of trouble to come, protests from some of the poorer Welsh who had lost their livelihoods since he had set up his fences, and some of the poor fools had threatened violence. Robert Dudley had had the same trouble when he was lord of Denbigh, Mister Smith assured him.

And then, into this scene of merriment came Sion, very conscious of his dignity. The visitor was announced.

'Mister Pendragon,' Gilbert repeated, and Nimue looked up from her place, her heart leaping in a sudden wild sensation into her throat so that it beat there, stopping her breath.

And here he was, dwarfing the softer, smoother men with his lean presence, his face stark above the crisp whiteness of a white shirt and black doublet, his cloak thrown back. Invited to join them, he graciously accepted a cup of wine but said he must return home without delay, he had come, with Mister Stoneyathe's permission, only to speak privately with Mistress Gwynne.

'You are acquainted?' Gilbert queried, frowning with some surprise towards Nimue, his gaze returning to the scarred face that met his steadily. It was evident that he was prepared to dislike Pendragon on sight, and his instinctive enmity was compounded by vague sensations of guilt, since he was well aware that some of the land he had enclosed within his new fences had long been worked by Pendragons and their tenants, grubbing some sort of a living from the poor hill soil. Ignatius Smith had been speaking only a moment previously of the prospect of summonses, warning Gilbert that the antagonism of his neighbours would do him little good, and Gilbert, with the obstinacy of the weak, was prepared to turn icily hostile if Pendragon had come to raise the subject of enclosures. Mention of Nimue had momentarily checked him.

'Perhaps you would care to ask the lady to enlighten you as to our relationship,' Pendragon suggested, with a slight, overly-courteous bow in Nimue's direction, and she rose hastily to her feet as the eyes of all turned towards her, pushing back her stool and clutching one hand in the folds of her velvet skirt, trying to stifle laughter.

'We are acquainted. I will speak with Mister Pendragon in the parlour,' she said, as composedly as she was able, and without waiting for Gilbert's acquiescence she led the way into the chamber bedecked for Christmas, where a cheerful fire was burning. Pendragon pushed closed the door against the plump, eager hovering of Morfydd with a tray, careless of proprieties, and turned to where Nimue stood breathless.

95

'You have come,' she managed, her delight shining in her eyes in spite of her efforts to remain cool and aloof. She looked enchanting. Her cheeks, as he commented after a moment returning her gaze, were pink and velvet like the damask rose.

'Oh, no, no, that was something my old friend Will Shakespeare would have kept as stock. You can turn a better compliment I am certain,' she laughed, joyous beyond imagining, raising her hands to the betraying flush.

'As to that, I have rarely been tested. Will you come with me? I have something to tell you,' he said, directly, and she faltered:

'Come – with you?'

Pendragon's firm mouth curved into a grin which made him appear suddenly very much younger.

'Seductions around every corner, is it? Keep your precious honour, then witch. Huw is preparing a feast to celebrate my natal day, and I would humbly request - .'

'Humbly?' Nimue said, laughing despite herself. 'No, never humbly. You could never be humble.'

He looked at her for a long moment, then: 'Could I not?' he asked, quietly, and she flushed again, shamed. 'I am sorry.'

'I wanted you with me,' he said simply. 'I could have carried you off, or sent spirits to bring you to me, witch, out-spelled you, but I thought you would prefer it this way. Will you gladden my house by sharing my birthday feast? And if you will, sleep safely in your chaste bed in my tower tonight. I will keep apart and return you unscathed to Stoneyathe tomorrow.'

Nimue drew in her breath, dazzled. She wanted to protest that she was not a child, that she did not have to be returned to Gilbert – and that in fact, the prospect of remaining unscathed did not altogether appeal to her. But she found herself saying instead, as though the words sprang from somewhere deep within her, and were drawn from her intuitively:

'What is *aur*?'

'*Aur*?' He seemed startled.

'Yes. I had a dream. It was the hermit, the man with the masked lantern, in the snow. He recognised me, and he told me.'

Pendragon reached out and took her by the shoulders, and she could feel the strength pouring from his hands, though they touched her only very gently.

'The hermit? God's blood, it was no hermit, witch, it was my father. It must have been so, for I too have found a sign, the same sign as you. Your vision, the dark cave, the words that were spoken, they were what he tried to tell me on the night of the fire. His legacy to me.'

His eyes were very dark, but there was something burning like a flame, deep within them. Nimue stood, at the reach of his hands.

'What is it?' she whispered. 'What is *aur*?'

He smiled then. 'Don't you know, witch? Where is your magic? *Aur* is gold.'

8

The candle flames softly touched starry points of light on the surface of the great globe of the heavens. Nimue stood within Pendragon's magical chamber, her cloak still about her shoulders, her fingers and toes tingling from the chill of the afternoon's ride through the wild, frosty air. It was Christmas, and though it was the first Yule feast she had celebrated without her father, she felt certain that Gereint Gwynne was at peace. As for herself – she was here with *him*, and she was so very alive that her body seemed to glow joyously in every limb.

In the yard outside the tower, huddled dark against the snows of the forest, they had alighted from their mounts and Pendragon had hurried her towards the ancient arched doorway that, open beneath the heavy fringing of thick icicles clinging to the stone-work above, promised warmth and cheer. He left the beasts to the care of a thin, hungry-looking gipsy of a lad who emerged from the buildings, his thatch of black coarse hair tumbling into his eyes.

'My new apprentice, Math,' Pendragon laughed as Nimue paused in surprise at the sight of the boy. 'He would learn to be a wizard and sure he has the very look of a changeling or an elf.'

Nimue smiled into the young face, brown as a nut with hazel eyes that were as deep as a well. The eyes, very like her own, smiled back at her without guile. She turned to Pendragon.

'And you will teach him?'

'I have told him he learns first to care better for the beasts than he does for himself, and to tend the herbs in my mother's little plot,' Pendragon replied easily. 'When he can see God in all things, however humble, then the wizardry will work of itself. He does not need teaching.'

Nimue felt a strong hand on her shoulder, guiding her towards the door of the tower. His touch seemed as though it burned even through her cloak. The very air was crisp and heightened with expectancy, and she found herself laughing a little breathlessly. Anything might happen this enchanted afternoon.

Ever since that moment when they had faced each other in the parlour at Grannah, and she had spoken of her dream of *aur*, which meant gold, a sense of high excitement had been mounting between them. His invitation itself had been the fabric of the most thrilling of adventures, but his words and her intuitive awareness of hidden mysteries still to be revealed seemed to have expanded the everyday realities for both of them far beyond the confines of the walls of Gilbert's house.

But even as Nimue would have spoken to him in the parlour, questioned him more closely about the vision, Pendragon had stilled her with a finger placed crosswise across her lips.

'Silence only is the best truth. Be silent, witch. Come with me, and I will tell you all.'

'I will fetch my cloak,' she rejoined quietly, and on eager feet she was gone from him. As she threw on her wolfskins, and her thick woollens for riding, her heart light within her breast, she thought that she would have gone with him without a word even if he had invited her to journey far beyond Pendragon tower, and on foot, to toil across the length and breadth of the world – anywhere so long as it was in his company.

And now, breathless from their ride, and with the warmth of the air within the chamber with its tapestries and outspread charts catching at her throat, she stood watching as Pendragon lifted something wrapped in a rough piece of dirty homespun from a small chest made of softest oiled wood, and gently pulled the cloth aside. He showed her what was so carefully hidden within.

'A piece of rock,' Nimue said, in surprise. 'What is it? Some strange crystal? Or just a rock, an old stone?'

'Look closer,' he invited, and handed her the object. It was cold to her touch, and glistened dully in the light. Then, suddenly, she caught the tiny flame of red-yellow, lapping up the stone. Gone even as she peered at it. She tilted the stone, really breathless now, and caught that flame of red-yellow again. There were veins spreading within the depths of its darkness, veins that, even in the candlelight, shone as nothing else upon this earth can shine.

'Gold. It is gold,' Nimue said dazedly, looking up at Pendragon, tearing her fascinated gaze from the threads of pure fire that held the shadows within the rock together. 'It is gold.' Her eyes were very wide. 'Is it the alchemist's stone? My father did not believe – oh, but then, John Dee and the rest were right. It is possible to live for ever, and to transmute base metal to gold.'

Pendragon reached a long arm across and gently took the cloth and its precious burden from her. He wrapped it again and replaced it in the chest, turning a small, but ornate key which he set deliberately upon the wooden table before him. Nimue, watching, saw the curve of his firm mouth set.

'It is not the alchemist's stone,' he said, and steered her towards a brazier that burned in the corner. 'My father too knew better than to trust to the wild stories of such as Nick Flamel, who they say was born into this world only to live immortal, able to create his own riches. There are many kinds of gold, and many kinds of immortality too. Your father was a man of wisdom. No, this is not magic nor created from the secrets of the Quabbalah, it is the true gold that is found in the earth, witch. Sit you, and we will refresh ourselves with mulled wine, and Huw will make ready the food, and I will tell you what I know. You are still cold, shivering. Warm yourself.'

Nimue sank down onto a three-legged stool, putting out her hands to the brazier. It was true that she was shivering, but it was not from cold now, though her cheeks were fiery red and her eyes bright from the ride through the crisp snowy air. She was quivering with excitement, with anticipation, with the joy of actually being within Pendragon tower with this man. And the rock with its golden veins and all the secrets it signified, the mystery of the visions, the words which had come to her, formless as the wind, the strange promise that hovered unseen as yet on the air, of glories to come, only added to her sense of reckless delight, heightened living and ecstatic abandonment.

Huw, silent in his white robes, was at her elbow, a goblet in his hands, and the sharp fragrance of cinnamon and something else, some Eastern drug she could not identify, reached her. The dark face with its light eyes smiled, and she realised she was thirsty. She took the goblet and drank the hot spiced wine, feeling it warm through her veins. She was not afraid of what strange potions there might be mixed within the cup. Here, there was only the power of the light, and Pendragon would let nothing harm her.

Her cloak was deftly removed, and she sat, warmth seeping through her, utterly at peace. She even felt her eyelids grow heavy and drowsed a little, saying nothing, content to wait until Pendragon might enlighten her. She would not ask foolish questions. He would, as he had said, tell her all when he thought fit to do so. The silence between them was familiar and easy, and wrapped Nimue like a soft quilt, warming her chilled bones all through. And after a while, Pendragon began to speak.

His long, lean body was relaxed in the only chair within the chamber, which was carved with heraldic beasts and symbols so that it had the appearance of a throne, his arms resting on the snarling heads of some ancient devils or demons, a cup held loosely in his own hand. His voice was quiet now, controlled, and the excitement that had driven them on their way from Grannah had been replaced by a soberness that shadowed his scarred face a little and was reflected in his measured words.

'My father scorned the wealth of this world, though he might have had wealth beyond the price of a kingdom, and he taught me to revere only the riches of the spirit. Yet the body must be fed as well as the soul, and he spoke sometimes of the priceless legacy he would leave to me when he went, though he would not let me know of it before.

'When he died, on the night of the fire, he tried to tell me something, but he could speak only with great difficulty, and I caught just a few words. They meant nothing then – but I told you this when you first came to me and recounted your message for me. Your message, your vision, it was the same. It was rich and strange, that message, like some invocation or spell – but you know this also because you have heard it. Again it meant nothing to me.

'On the night of the fire when my father was dying, I knew only that I could not save him. The struggle to speak took all his failing strength, but it was for naught, I was not listening and he was gone within a few more breaths.'

Nimue was silent. She could see it all in her mind's eye, the ruined wreck of the house, the fallen masonry and charred wood still smouldering as the red fingers of dawn streaked the eastern sky, as though angry at the destruction it beheld. A terrible sadness swept over her, but she recognised that it was not her own, it was the sadness and reproachfulness Pendragon carried within himself, in the manner of a son, when he recalled the death of his father.

'The house burned,' she said, looking round her at the peaceful chamber. 'Did you then built it again with magic?'

'Hardly,' he replied, the shadows on his face lifting a little. 'These walls have been standing since the days of Arthur, they say. There have been Pendragons time out of mind, and those who are aware have always come to us, prince and pauper alike, for richness has nothing to do with wealth as the world would measure it. Even Elizabeth's emissaries have found their way here – oh yes,' he told her, smiling a little at her surprise. 'The Queen is well aware of the powers beyond the temporal, and she has had dealings with many of the wise in all parts of her kingdom, not just John Dee and your father. Remember the year of the Armada, when we feared for this island itself, that it would fall beneath the Spanish boot?'

Nimue nodded, her eyes wide and grave.

'Indeed. I helped my father to call on the powers, at the Queen's earnest behest. He worked for three nights and days in defence of the realm.'

'All of us did the same,' Pendragon assured her. 'On the wild moors, on the hills and in all the villages, the wise men and wise women fought as they had never fought before to avert the Spanish threat. I too, here, did what my own father would have done. We were companions in arms then, you and I. The temporal world does not matter to those who are aware of the spirit, but for the minds that still grope their way, it is necessary that certain orders must be maintained – and this land was not meant to fall beneath the sway of Spain.'

Nimue nodded slowly. She had heard her father say the same, when the great fleet of the Armada had sailed and the time of crisis had loomed, and she had been scarcely out of childhood, yet important enough to assist him as he worked with the powers to defend England against the invader.

Pendragon sighed.

'My father had been gone years by then. It was not the tower but the house on the far side of the yard that burned when the fire happened. And the ruins remain there still, part of the earth, one with the ivy and the gentle weeds and plants with which nature softens and mends her scars, in time. The house was naught but a bothy, what they call a *ty unnos* here, that had housed cottagers, and often their beasts too. But there was a fine hearth, slate, quarried not far away from here, and since it was bitter cold in the tower, and damp, I made the place my father's Dower House. The rheums were in his old bones, nor could they be healed, and I would not let him perish within these walls, but set him keeping warm before the fire, sitting there with Huw to wait on him in his last days, looking over his garden, for he could not stir without help, not in those last months.'

He made a gesture of impatience, restrained but touching in its intensity.

'On the night of the fire, I had to go to him from this chamber, where I was working on a chart. The tower was hardly touched, but the house burned like a torch, there was a wind from the north, and it was soon gone, and he with it. He could not escape, you see. Huw was with me, and my father had been sleeping, but he had been caught by the smoke, trying to crawl, when I found him.'

Nimue still said nothing, though the horror of that old tragedy touched her like a cold hand. Then she found herself speaking, words that seemed to come from a far distance into her mind.

'Do not torment yourself. He does not suffer. It is your suffering only, like the night mare, which you must ride again and again. In truth, he is at peace, freed from the confines of his twisted joints and the weight of his years. He is straight again, youthful as you never knew him. The fire opened the gate for him, and he was glad to go. He had long been waiting until the Wyrd was spun.'

The words hung softly in the chamber and Pendragon seemed about to answer, then he turned as Huw bowed in the doorway, his hands thrust within his long white sleeves. Caught between Nimue's eyes and the inscrutable gaze of the silent man, Pendragon appeared to stir and throw off the weight of his melancholy, as though shrugging away a dark, heavy cloak. His face was enlivened, lit with new fire as he addressed Nimue.

'It is done. Huw has the feast prepared for us, witch, and it is time for me to let go the past. Huw has long waited for this, he did not sorrow over my father's going, he has the certainty of his wisdom. But I was my father's son and I could not see him pass from me easily. I raged against the fate that had taken him – but now indeed, he speaks through you, to shame me.'

Nimue would have cried out in impulsive protest at those low words, to tell him that there was no shame, that there could never be shame in loving, but he made a gesture and she thought better of it. He went on, rising and looking directly at her: 'He is at rest, and this is the celebration of my natal day.'

He paused, while the hot blood flamed to her cheeks once more.

'And on this day of days you, my witch, are with me. To sit at my table and take wine from my cup and food from my trencher. My lady, you are welcome indeed. Your place is waiting for you, and has been these many long years.'

He held out his hand, and formally, as though performing the stylised steps of a dance, Nimue too rose and moved a pace towards him. He had the look more than ever of some ancient princeling, in his dark burgundy velvet and slashed sleeves, and his head was bent with restrained passion towards her. The moment seemed poised between past and future, as had the moment before Nimue had knocked for the first time on the door of the tower. It hung, breathlessly. Then she moved, deliberately placed her fingers in his, looking up all the while into his face.

She seemed to be watching from some vantage point outside of her self. She could see her own figure, slender as a birch sapling in her black bodice, the skin of her neck gleaming palely and her head held proudly above the white collar that lay in fine threads of cobwebby lace across her shoulders. Her gown was by no means as fine as Mary's satins, and the collar was one she had worked herself. But the soft curls of her hair clung about her head like the petals of some small dark flower, the top of it level with Pendragon's shoulder. There was something yielding, yet resolute as steel, in her bearing that marked her intangibly as her own father's daughter. Something mysterious and fey, as though she had not been born in the manner of all flesh, but that the other Welsh wizard had conjured her, through magic, from the shadowy pools in the forest and formed her creamy skin from petals of hawthorn blossom.

Pendragon was staring fixedly at her as though he was held beneath a spell. She only could set him free. Nimue moved, passing before him in silence from the chamber to go to the feast.

Their departure from Grannah had not been accomplished without incident. Gilbert had indicated coldly that he considered Pendragon's unexpected arrival and invitation – and indeed, her own willingness to accept it, considering the fact that the family were already seated at the festive board themselves – in doubtful taste, but he had accepted her apologies and graciously permitted her to withdraw. None of the company seated so merrily in the hall at Grannah had ever before encountered such a situation, they sat open-mouthed as though they were at a fair, and Nimue thought rather wryly that the account of Pendragon's startlingly dramatic entry into the feast, her own rising from table and leaping (for so Will Shakespeare might have phrased it, allowing his poetic imagination some license) into the saddle to ride away with him to Pendragon tower, all this, in intense detail, would pass into the realms of legend. One more tale like that of the Mistletoe Bough, to be told to wide-eyed children over the chestnuts on the blazing Christmas hearth, in years to come.

It seemed that whatever she might try to do to avoid notice, yet fate sought her out. And as for Pendragon, well, she could conceive of no way in which his path had not been marked by significant stars that blazed across the heavens of his chart in fiery trails from the moment of his birth.

'You are your own mistress,' Gilbert told Nimue, when she informed him quietly of Pendragon's invitation to mark the Yule feast within his tower, and the fact that she would, as soon as her pony was ready, be going with him, to return on the morrow.

He looked at her flushed face with a slight shifting of his brows, eyeing her with more attention than he had paid her for many a week. This new development – and the appearance from nowhere of an unexpected admirer – had kindled his fascination with her again, and he found himself suddenly seeing her through new eyes, wanting what he had rejected and now could not have. But rather than admit it, he took refuge in the amazement of Mary and their guests, who were still sitting at table, arrested in mid-feast, anxious to watch goggle-eyed whatever scandals might occur. And the appearance of one of the most surly local misogynists, a man whose very face spoke of dealings that were best not investigated in the light of day, apparently coming a-courting a woman of doubtful ante-cedents, not to mention known witchlike propensities – all this was the stuff of the most spectacular of scandals to have occurred in the neighbourhood for years.

'It is not for me to question your wisdom nor your desires,' Gilbert smiled, though the smile touched his lips only. His eyes were hard. 'You have worked faithfully for me and my house and kept your part of our bargain, and you have earned your dues. Take your holy day with my blessing, Nimue, and spend it how you will. And,' he added so softly that she wondered for a moment whether he had really spoken the words, 'the night also. I might have expected no more than this from you, your father's daughter.'

There was a moment of stillness. Nimue's anger stirred so that her body would have moved in retaliation, except that she seemed to feel her father's restraining hand almost physically upon her shoulder. Such an insult would have provoked anyone, man or woman, to challenge Gilbert, to strike him, even. And even he seemed aware that he had gone too far. There was a wariness to his mouth. Then:

'Thank you, Gilbert,' Nimue responded with deliberate sweetness, choosing not to acknowledge the insult. The words reflected what was in his mind, not the truth. But all the same, she was hoping fervently that Pendragon had not heard them. She added with as much dignity as she could muster: 'I will return tomorrow, not to neglect your household.'

He did not answer, but turned to address Pendragon with frigid politeness, though in view of his previous remark, his words were singularly unapt.

'Be careful for Mistress Gwynne, Mister Pendragon, she is in my trust.'

And suddenly, Nimue knew without a doubt that Pendragon had indeed been aware of that cruel little shaft. But, quicker than herself but deadlier, he knocked it away as skilfully as though it had been a blow from a swung daisy-chain. Lightly, almost insultingly, he returned Gilbert's bow.

'I will care for her,' he promised, so insinuatingly that Nimue, in the shifting of the atmosphere to hilarity, almost laughed aloud, 'as though she were my own.'

But as Nimue went from the hall, Pendragon turned back and said in a different tone to Gilbert:

'Gwilym the Stone and his family will be leaving the Cwm tonight to look for work, and Cait is near her time. I told them the fences must and would come down, Stoneyathe. There are no fences across Pendragon land, nor across the lands around Caercerrig or Gwenallt nor the rest of the mountain neither. It has been worked by all, time immemorial, there is no gentry and common, no master of Grannah and landless here. I warn you before others take matters into their own hands, and they will not be so punctilious as myself. Less squeamish, them. They have nothing to lose, you see.'

Once more, as so often during conversations in which Gilbert took part, the silence froze for a long moment, then Gilbert said with finely calculated affectation that, with his lifted brows, was an insult in itself:

'I am familiar with the name of Gwilym the Stone of course, he is a tenant of Grannah, dwelling within my boundaries. But I fail to see what he has to do with you, Mister Pendragon, nor why you should take it upon yourself to speak for him. The running of this estate is no concern of any except myself and my appointed men of business.'

He paused briefly, so that Pendragon might have answered him with hot words if he had had a mind to do so, but there was no reaction, and after a moment, Gilbert gave a slight shrug and continued:

'My cousin David might have chosen to conduct his affairs in a very different manner, but I have found since I took over the estate that there are criminal irregularities that have been perpetuated in the past which must, and will be corrected. The man is regrettably unable, like many another, to meet his fair and reasonable rent. It is long overdue, years in fact I believe. No estate can be run on charity, but I have had the kindness to give them leave to stay until the child is born.'

There was another silence. Then:

'It would be kinder to take down the fences. There are others, with families and livings to make.'

Pendragon's voice was even, but the silent guests at the board, looking at Gilbert, saw a red light touch his narrowed eyes, and the leap of the muscle at the side of his jaw.

'Is this formal business, on a feast day, Mister Pendragon? Come to me tomorrow if you would inform me of your interest in Grannah and plead the case for Gwilym the Stone and his like, and I will discourse with you then. My sister - ,' Gilbert indicated a wide-eyed Mary, who was watching suspiciously, already scandalised by Nimue's withdrawal from the table, and suspecting that there was some further undercurrent to the conversation, but unable to decide exactly what it was. 'My sister is a lady, accustomed to the manners of polite society.'

Pendragon bowed once more, briefly, towards Mary.

'My deepest reverences, madam. Pray excuse the uncivil behaviour that clouds your festive board this merry morning. And - ,' he added very softly, 'the uncivil man who is the cause of it.'

Mary, magnetised by his presence, feeling herself drowning in the depths of his dark eyes, squeaked back readily enough that of course she forgave him, but for some reason she did not understand, Gilbert shot a glare of white-hot fury towards her, and brusquely ordered her to leave Mister Pendragon take his departure. With Mary, Mistress Emma and Ignatius Smith watching uneasily, Pendragon strode from the hall and out into the snowy yard where Nimue joined him in a few moments, wrapped in her cloak and furs. They were both in the saddle in a few minutes, and Pendragon was riding ahead of her into the trees.

And so, she thought as they made their white way through the afternoon to Pendragon, I have lost my respectability – I have thrown it to the winds, and the world will say with Gilbert, that I am the daughter of a wizard, and they would have expected nothing else from me. But as she rode with the dark shape of Pendragon on his white horse picking a path before her, Nimue felt a blaze of exhilaration seize her. Wizards' daughters, at any rate, were not afraid to live. Nor wizards' sons, either. She counted Gilbert and Mary, Mistress Emma and Ignatius Smith and Dorabella and their world well lost for this moment of sheer delight filled with a glorious awareness of the abundance of life.

But later, in the sanctuary that the walls of Pendragon tower offered to those who found their way by whatever enchantment within, relaxed and warmed as she sat with Pendragon at the feast and ate companionably, he turned his attention to deeper matters.

'Those words my father spoke, the words you have told me, they do not refer to the transmuting of gold from base metal,' he told Nimue. 'It is quite clear – the gold itself is to be found in the earth, to be mined perhaps. Think, there are mines everywhere in these hills, why, on Halkyn Mountain, there have been lead mines since before the Legions came and went. And if lead and metals such as copper, then why not gold? This, I am sure, was my father's legacy, that he kept so closely from me, almost until it was too late.'

'You mean – that rock is from a mine? There is gold somewhere near here, to be mined?' she breathed, thrilled beyond measure. 'But would not it be known?'

'My father knew,' he said, frowning. 'He must have known. He knew where the rock came from, and he kept it in that little chest, which I never saw before until two nights ago. Math was picking stones in the ruins of the burned house, and he found it lying unharmed in the debris. And, God's teeth, with the key still in the lock. How is that for a chance, a mad, wild chance, witch?'

Nimue stared at him, once again seeming to hear her father's voice, as she had heard it so many times when he was alive, low and resonant with certainty.

'But there is no chance,' she said, her eyes shining. 'Only the working out of fate. You are a wizard's son, you must know it is so.'

'Indeed, I do,' Pendragon agreed. He lifted his goblet to her. 'And I know too that there is always a time and a moment, and that mine has waited on you and your coming, witch.'

Nimue, looking at the light catching the silvery sheen of the cup, felt her senses quiver into new awareness. Superimposed on her view of the chamber with its meats and sweetmeats spread for the delectation, the handiwork of the silent Huw, she seemed to see the bleak hillside of her dream, and the dark figure of the hermit with his masked lantern. Again she heard his voice, and without conscious volition, she repeated the words aloud, falteringly.

'*Dyma 'n awr. Ac aur. Awr,*' she murmured, and Pendragon's voice sharpened, cutting into the image so that it fled and only the chamber was there again.

'What words are those?'

'The hermit, in my dream. He blessed me, and that is what he said,' Nimue told him, and Pendragon looked at her long and hard, an expression of awe and wonder lightening his ravaged face, filling it with light.

'*The hour is come. And the gold. It is time.*'

'My father spoke to me of the gold as he was dying, but the time was not opportune. Then he waited until you came, and told you so that you might tell me also. But still it was not the time, and so I did not understand. Now, though, he has guided Math's foot to stumble on the chest, the little chest he had hidden and could not give me himself. There it is, witch. Clear as the day. There is gold to be found somewhere in this earth, that rock is veined with it – and my father knew where it was. He intended it as my inheritance, and so *ipso facto*, it must be on Pendragon land.'

111

'He was right to keep silent,' Nimue said slowly. She regarded Pendragon with grave, candid eyes. 'The power of gold is very great. It can drive men to madness. If anyone knew – if Gilbert knew, for instance - .' She drew in her breath sharply. 'He would go wild with fever for it.'

'No-one knows, and they will not know,' Pendragon said coolly. ' But my father intended us to find out the truth. Us, you and I together. Before you came, there were long years when the chest must have been lying almost at my feet, and I did not see it. The words, also, were known to me and I did not understand them. But my father gave you the vision that revealed the truth, and he gave young Math the eyes to see the chest, not me.' He gestured briefly, with a half-smile. 'He thought of everything. He gave the boy an honest heart, so that he brought it to me.'

Nimue shivered suddenly, turning away.

'I wish it had not been gold,' she said, very low. 'I have seen what it does to men at Court, and how it can change them into beasts, slavering.'

'No, not the gold,' he told her gently, watching her. 'It is not the gold that does that, but the lust for gold, the desire to possess it. Gold is the most precious of metals, filled with rare power to uplift, to inspire, to transform, to heal.' He paused, looking down at the fine linen cloth which covered the festive board.

'My father had his reasons, else he would not have waited until you came, witch. I have been given the gold now that I have, perhaps, been able to acquire the wisdom to rejoice at the gift and take my pleasure in sharing it with another. If indeed there is gold, if there is metal to be found and mined, it is not meant for me alone. Here.' He reached within his doublet and held something across to her. It gleamed dully in the light of the candle flames.

'The key?' Nimue said, bewildered. 'The key to the chest?'

'Take it,' Pendragon urged her. 'It is yours. I make you a gift of it.'

Nimue felt as though she had wandered into some wispy haze of a dream far beyond the scene of the Christmas feast at Pendragon tower. She was silent, not knowing what to answer.

'If there is gold,' Pendragon repeated, and his voice compelled her, as did his eyes, burning darkly into hers, 'if there is gold, yours is the key to find it, and the chest itself with the rock within it, the proof, the evidence that such gold exists. I entrust it to your keeping.'

'But – that is foolish. It may be the wealth of the Indies, such as Drake and those like him brought back from their voyages for the Queen,' Nimue protested, wondering for a wild moment if he was mad.

'Even so,' Pendragon agreed, and smiled. The smile touched his scars with such sweetness that Nimue's heart contracted, then beat hard, sending the blood to her head. 'It is the best I have to give you. I would give you the stars to hang about your neck, moons to deck your hair, witch, save that you have no need of them, for your eyes are the brightest of jewels. If there is gold, take it for your portion, and make it into a ring to wear on your finger. I have always thought fine to wed with a lady of great wealth.'

She choked, aware that he was laughing, mocking her.

'W – wed?' she echoed, unable to say more.

'Why should we not wed, witch? In the eyes of Stoneyathe, you are as good as wed, unless you are a wanton. We have known this since the beginning.' There was a sudden flicker of doubt in his voice. 'I at least have known it must be so. The world will expect it, and - I would not have you leave me again.'

The moment, the time, Nimue thought dazedly, had become entangled with times of long past, she was aware of echoes of other meetings and other partings. But they would not be parted now. Feeling her joy rising as though on bright wings, lifting her with it, she tried to speak coolly and calmly.

'You wish to wed with me, Mister Pendragon?'

'Ah, witch, will you torment me?' he teased, mock-sighing. 'I must wed you, whether I wish it or not. For your sake, for your good name only. Otherwise, the honest matrons and fine ladies of county society will not let you sit in their august presence in church, they will not pronounce judgement on your puddings and pasties nor inform you for hours in the most awful detail of the sufferings of the childbed and all the other trials of their feminine existence. You will be no woman like them, a goodwife, but an outcast, a harlot, a poor creature who had not the wiles to entrap a husband. And do not speak to them of loving, nor of soul-mating with one who has waited faithfully for you a long lifetime, they do not know of such things. I cannot condemn you to such a life, deprived of the comforts of your sex.'

Nimue's hand was at her mouth, she was laughing delightedly at the picture his words created.

'Poof, I do not care a fig about puddings and pasties and sitting in church with them, Mistress Emma and Dorabella and the rest.'

'Even so,' he said softly. 'I care. I do not want to see you shamed before the world, however little that world means to me. We must live in it, my witch, and it is a small enough thing I can do to keep your name honest. That is,' he added, rather desperately, 'if the name of Pendragon can ever be aught but linked with the devil in county gossip.'

The name of Pendragon. It sounded to Nimue like the sound of a great horn, or trumpet. Pendragon. *She* would be a Pendragon. More than ever certain she was in a dream, she said:

'But – when should we wed? – And – where – and how?'

'I have thought of this for some time,' Pendragon admitted. 'This is a blessed day and a blessed night, none better for a wedding. We could be wed tonight, at the holy shrine above the well of Saint Mary, the hermit will perform the ceremony.'

114

Nimue looked into his eyes. They were shining as though they would reflect the light that his words had kindled in her own.

'My father used to say, the better the day, the better the deed,' she declared demurely. 'So if we were to heed his counsel – we should indeed be wed – tonight.'

9

And so on a night of frost and stars, the hills lowering dark-white in the black of night and sky, water tinkling everywhere as though the very ice flowed, the warmth of their beasts beneath them, foggy breaths hanging in snorting clouds of life, they came at last to the chapel above the holy spring beside the Elwy. The winter dawn was kindling sparks of red in the eastern sky, as Nimue became a Pendragon.

Later, when she was able to calculate the positions of the stars and planets, she saw that the heavens themselves had poured bounty upon them, for at the hour when she and Pendragon were wedded, Venus was in the seventh house, and Jupiter filling the whole horizon, signifying love and joy. Nimue did not need such reassurance for she knew intuitively that her whole life had been leading her to the candlelit gloom of the chapel above the well of Saint Mary – in Pendragon's deep, rich voice, in the tongue Nimue would consider her own twice over now, *y fynnon Fair*. Everything she had ever striven for had been just a preparation for the moment when, shivering in her cloak, but with her hand warmly clasped in Pendragon's, she stood with him before the old man with the saintly eyes who had, at Pendragon's urgent request, consented to marry them.

For as soon as Pendragon had spoken of marriage, they had fallen silent, and had sat looking at each other, all settled between them. Then he roused himself and gave a half-shrug, turning away.

'Ah, but it would be a long, hard ride, my witch, and hours in a cold saddle. In the spring, the winter babes will be taken to the shrine for baptising, but lovers who would wed in December must brave the wild ways and suffer. The holy brother is always there, and he will marry us if we are to go to him, but afterwards, if you are to keep your word to Stoneyathe and return to Grannah, we cannot linger, but must mount again, and ride. So there will be a wedding but no bridebed for you, not until you can come to me as my lady and my wife.'

He paused, looking at her downcast eyes, then went on huskily: 'Or else, let us keep our wits about us, and marry when the Beltane fires are lit and all the world is wedded. We will stay warm tonight and fill up our cups together, and you shall sleep in your virginal bed in the tower, for I would not dishonour you for the world, though you drive me to distraction with just the sight of you and the sound of your voice. I would not have you think your intended husband a ravisher.'

Nimue lifted her head. Her face was radiant with happiness, and filled with mischief.

'Oh, you know as well as I that if we filled up our cups and stayed warm, we should be doing the opposite of keeping our wits about us, sir. Let us be reckless, let us go to the holy brother now, as soon as we may,' she said, and added with laughter bubbling through her voice, 'Though I would make no protest at being ravished, if it was you who ravished me.'

Pendragon turned away in mock-despair. He drew a quick breath and then reached out, seizing her hand.

'Do not torment me, my witch, or else there will be no bother with wedding, but I will carry you in my arms to the tower, and in the morning you will upbraid me and say you cannot marry a man who has no will of his own, but is in thrall to a little slip of a wench's eyes.'

'I will never upbraid you,' Nimue declared with spirit.

116

'A saint, is it?' he teased, touching the soft curls above her forehead caressingly. 'Oh, no, but you will always spit fire, my lady, as you did when first we met on the seastrand. Or else there will be no wedding. For I will not marry with a saint.'

Their laughter was something new and wonderful, shared between them and ringing out merrily as a song. Excitedly, Nimue pleaded:

'Oh, let us not wait, let us go, tell Math to saddle the beasts. We have not come so far and had all settled so long ago when our moons eclipsed on the south nodes, to stop and think sense now. Nothing can harm us or stand in our way. Let us be gone.'

So they rode through the night with Math, risking life and limb in the deep mired valleys and through drifts where the horses stumbled and all appeared lost more times than they could count. But it seemed to Nimue as though their beasts possessed winged hooves that flew, speedily eating up the miles. The hills laid their highways open for the little party, and she wondered whether it was her father or the wizard, or both of them, who was with them speeding them on their flight through the night.

There were spirits pressing around them everywhere in the dark, and the sense of still wonder, and to Nimue the most powerful magic was in the figure of Pendragon himself, tall and black beside her, or riding ahead with Math on his sturdy little Welsh pony, carrying a flaring pine knot for a torch.

It was a time of such enchantment that Nimue would not have been surprised if she had heard the echo of the angelic host singing the *Gloria. In excelsis*, she thought jubilantly, as she rode, ecstatic and uncaring, to her wedding.

She took no heed of the cramped hours in the saddle, the cold numbing her fingers and toes, her nose red and shining, her gown and cloak soaked and smirched from that wild ride, her limbs drooping with sheer weariness. It was little enough to pay for the moment when, as the new day smouldered into crimson in the eastern sky, the words were spoken which would unite them until death and the old monk lifted his hand, pronouncing the blessing.

They swore their vows, in the old tradition, on the hilt of Pendragon's sword, and when it was done, Pendragon turned to Nimue in the little chapel, with the incense smoky about them, and took her hungrily in his arms, saying on a low, ragged breath:

'Ah, witch.'

He bent his head and kissed her, and she reached up, clinging joyously, giving him back kiss for kiss, tasting the sweetness of his lips like wild honey until at last, for shame's sake since they were in a holy place, they drew reluctantly apart.

The old monk had been waiting, gravely patient, with his hands folded in the wide sleeves of his robe. He could see how Nimue shivered, in spite of the blaze of joy in her green-gold eyes, as she looked up at her husband, and Pendragon's long arm around her shoulders, pulling her close to him as though he would never let her go.

'And is this the way you will treat your lady, my son, chill her to the bone?' the old man said reprovingly to Pendragon. 'Is it a warrior to follow you to the wars that you are after? Tck, tck, but she is only a maid, and like all men you will bring her trouble enough in the future, let her be easy for now. There is fire in my cell, and a restorative to warm her.'

'We have troubled you enough this night,' Pendragon replied reluctantly, for though he was fiercely proud of the loyal and faithful endurance Nimue had displayed during the long ride, he would have given his own food and rest for half a year in order that she should now eat and sleep.

'Is there some inn? Some house?' he asked, thinking to send Math ahead to make some provision for Nimue's comfort, but the old man smiled slowly, his face crinkling into wrinkles.

'Inns are for others,' he said. 'For you and your lady, your devotion is an inn where you may rest and take your ease. Oh, she will tread a harder road than this as your goodwife, Mister Pendragon, I do not doubt. Bring her to my cell.'

Nimue was white-faced but radiant, holding tightly to Pendragon's hand.

'The good brother is right,' she said, with shining eyes. 'Inns are for other people. We do not need an inn. I can ride on – husband.'

He turned on her then, scowling fearsomely, touched to the heart by her words and her look of sweet pride.

'As my wife, you will obey me, witch,' he growled. 'And it is my wish that you learn to leave off clacking and do what your betters tell you. I say you will go with the good brother and take his magnanimous hospitality and restore yourself and rest.'

In the end, with Math in attendance, they both sat beside the fire in the monk's sparse cell and feasted on smoked mutton and sops in milk and ale for their wedding breakfast, unable to stop smiling at each other as they ate. They were hungry after their ride, and it would be many hours before Nimue could satisfy her hunger again, so Pendragon pressed her to the food and drink the old man provided, then the holy brother led Nimue to his own pallet and bade her rest. With Math keeping watch, she slept, while Pendragon went with their host to the chapel for mass. He knelt on the cold flags, pledging himself anew to his bride, and thinking deep thoughts he had not yet shared with her, for there had been no time.

But before they departed, talk they must, for there were things that needed to be said, and they could not speak as they rode.

'I promised you that you would sleep the night in your virginal bed and return to Stoneyathe untouched,' he said, looking down at her, and she sat up, warm and flushed with slumber, pulling her knees up to her chest, her arms wound round them, resting her chin on her clasped hands. The fur Math had placed round her shoulders framed her face in tawny gold.

'And so I will,' she laughed up at him. 'For I have slept chastely beneath the auspices of the holy church, and you have not touched me.'

'Ah, witch,' Pendragon said regretfully, half-pleading. 'You know I would not have it so.'

And now there was matching desire in her own eyes.

'Nor would I,' she said candidly. 'But I gave my word to Gilbert, and there are the duties of the house that I must see to at Grannah, I cannot leave the household to Mary's tender care. I took the responsibility on myself, as you know, and I will not neglect it.'

She paused, smiling, then went on shyly: 'But on this glorious day, is it not enough that we two are wedded? I want to sing out my thanks to the spirit that watches over us for giving me such blessings as your love and your name, and your presence here with me. My father used to say that there should be temperance in all things, and that too much joy was as bad as none. It is enough – oh, it is everything, that I am a Pendragon now, and your wife. I am sure the women who were of this proud lineage before me did not sniff and snivel about their lot. They were wise, they knew how to keep their counsel and wait until the moment came. And come it will. I love you with all my heart, my dearest husband, and I would never part from you, but if I must leave you for a little while, for the sake of my word, then I will be patient and wait.'

Pendragon leaned close and took her hands.

'Come back with me now,' he said, passionate and low, his wise intentions all forgotten and she laughed with delight, clasping his fingers between her own. But then the laughter faded, and she turned her face away, becoming grave. She too had things that must be said.

'I would come to you and let them all go hang, but it is not just my word that takes me back to Grannah,' she confessed. 'I am afraid of Gilbert, not for myself but for you.'

Pendragon too shook off his mad mood and settled himself beside her, his lithe back leaning easily against the stone. He frowned, and his face became very stern. The light of the candle softly touched his scars.

'Yes, you see true, my witch. Stoneyathe will indeed bear watching. He is not only full of greed but he is weak, and such a combination can be dangerous.'

'Since he came to Grannah, he has changed. He is mad for land to add to the estate, and he has already instructed Mister Smith to file claims in the courts,' Nimue said, frowning also. 'I have heard him talking to Dorabella about it, and she is his bad angel, she feeds his ambition. But he is not a man to be satisfied at making proper application through the courts, he will take what he wants, caring nothing, and if you stand against him he will make an enemy of you. He has already maimed one man with his mantraps. He is cold, Gilbert, and shows no mercy. He has put people out of their homes - .'

'I know,' he said quietly. 'I spoke to him before we left Grannah.'

'Then it will be dangerous for you,' Nimue said urgently. 'Some of it is Pendragon land he has taken, half the mountain. And,' she added, low, 'if he should hear of the gold - .'

'No-one will know of the gold until I am ready to tell them,' Pendragon assured her evenly. 'Gilbert Stoneyathe is naught but a petty tyrant, my witch, what power do you think he wields against that of the owl, the snake and the spider? I have no fear of him, I have lived all my life at Pendragon and I can charm the very rocks. It is for those like Gwilym the Stone and his wife and their unborn child that I am angered. And you too, now that we are wedded, Pendragon is your home, and Pendragon land is your land. If he knows that you are my wife, his devious mind might try to strike at me through you.'

'I will not tell him,' Nimue declared after a moment, when she had lost herself in the delirious prospect he had mentioned, still so new to her, that she had, as well as a husband, gained a home and a heritage to uphold as a woman of Pendragon. It was a prospect that was breathtaking, like coming out of a dark room into the bright sunlight. Her father had indeed seen true when he had prophesied that she would find her destiny, her self and her heart's desire, in the west. 'I will tell no-one. I do not doubt your power, but I know that he is dangerous – and in spite of me, I know that the danger is for you.'

She shivered suddenly, unable to repress a momentary stab of dark awareness blotting out the images around her. There was dark – there was darkness that surrounded Pendragon like a cloud, hanging in the air, the dark of disaster and fear, of terror and death.

'I must stay at Grannah,' she said urgently. 'I must know of his plans, so that I can protect you. It is the only way. I can watch and listen, so that you may be warned in time if he should strike out at you. He wants your land and he will take your gold if he knows of it. God's blood, he would kill you without compunction for such a prize.'

'I was born to die peacefully in my bed, an ancient with toothless gums mumbling my prayers,' her husband teased, and she smiled unwillingly, troubled but unable to resist the picture his words conjured up. 'But we must be wise, witch,' he went on gravely, 'since the gold is your marriage settlement, for you to wear on your slender fingers or around your sweet neck, and to keep you when you are a dowager, dozing beside the hearth with grandsons and their infants tip-toeing lest they should wake the fearsome old lady of Pendragon.'

He frowned again, grave. 'I do not know enough of the mining of metals.'

'And I know nothing, only their properties that my father taught me,' Nimue added.

'We must consult with one skilled in such things,' he went on, pausing to consider. 'There is a man, well known to all the miners on Halkyn Mountain – and that is not far to the north from here, where there have been workings as I told you, since the beginning of time. He was a friend of my father, a colleague also, a man of great wisdom in ancient lore as well as the working of metals, which is his love and his life. I will send Math to him with a message and ask him to come to Pendragon as soon as he may. He will come, for my father's sake. There are parchments in the chest, I cannot interpret them save only roughly, and when I show him the rock and the parchments with it, we will know more.'

He paused again, then said thoughtfully: 'There are many old workings on the mountain, on other land as well as Pendragon, even on Grannah, but all of them long since worked out, so it has been thought. But if any man will know the truth of it, it is Owain ab Owain. Him too, we can trust. Like my father, he cares naught for the riches of this world.' Then, smiling a little crookedly, he told her:

'I must take back the key of the chest so that Owain can unlock it, my pretty.'

Nimue reached up to lift the precious key, which Pendragon had slung on a thin chain of silver for her to wear round her neck, and as she did so, her fingers touched the little cross made of iron horseshoe nails, which had hung on its silken thread since she was a tiny child. Impulsively, she lifted them both over her head, and held them out to him.

'You may have the key and welcome, for you have made me rich beyond imagining already. Your very presence is the alchemy that has transformed my life – I need no philosopher's stone for it will remain so until the day I die. But I want to give you a wedding gift in return. Take this token and wear it for me, to protect you as it has protected me all my life, since my father gave it to me. It has the power of the cross, and of iron which is the master of all metals, and it has seen the prayers and passions of my soul as I grew to womanhood, struggling to hold fast to the light. Take it and wear it so that it may protect you when I am not beside you, and also in your searching for the metals deep within the earth.'

Pendragon held the little cross reverently, then lifted it to his lips.

'It is warm from your breast,' he said huskily. 'I will wear it against my heart until I can hold you there in very truth. And now - .' He spoke deliberately, so that the atmosphere between them lost its close intimacy. 'We must ride, my witch. I will return you to Grannah, to Stoneyathe, and as soon as I may, I will be with you. Or else Math will bring a message. It will not be long, I promise you, before we will be together.'

They parted late in the evening, embracing passionately in the light of a gold crescent moon that was tangled in the bare twigs of the forest trees, half-sunk in snow on the wild hillside a mile from Grannah. Then, decorously, they rode at last into the yard, and the dogs set up their howling and barking and one of the men came running out to take Nimue's pony, which was stumbling now, exhausted, though they had kept an easy pace through the day for the sake of the beasts.

Nimue slid stiffly from the saddle, turning as a warm, bright swathe of torchlight was flung into the yard from the great door. She saw Gilbert standing there peering out, with Mary's sharp-featured little face pushed over his shoulder. They were in their festive finery, and Nimue recollected somewhat dazedly that this was the second day of Christmas, and that they were still celebrating the festival they had all celebrated so many times in the past, at Court or in the little house near London Bridge, in a world that seemed lifetimes away from them now. She marvelled at how much further she herself had journeyed since she had last seen them, through night and place and time to some far star, the candles burning at a holy shrine, to be transformed from maiden to wife – even if it was only wife in name to Pendragon as yet.

There was no sign of Ignatius Smith and his sister, and she realised they must have departed as they had planned. But Dorabella was at Gilbert's elbow, a kind of tight, secretive triumph in her bearing. And as Nimue looked, she placed one hand deliberately on his arm.

'I have returned as I promised, Gilbert,' Nimue said, with as much self-possession as she could muster. She turned back to look up at Pendragon. 'Mister Stoneyathe would be obliged, I know, if you would take a cup of wine and some refreshment before your ride back to Pendragon, after your care of me, sir.'

This was entirely for the benefit of the avid watchers, for they had already decided that it would be best if he left immediately, since his white horse, like the powerful beast it was, had not yet even begun to flag. Gilbert's suggestion that he should formally represent his interests in the affairs of Grannah and that of those who had been dispossessed by the enclosing of the common and wild land had been, they had agreed, merely a wordy gesture. Gilbert was not prepared even to listen, far less to consider such representations seriously. In view of everything, they had agreed, the less Gilbert and Pendragon saw of each other from this day on, the better.

'Though,' Pendragon told Nimue, with lines of concern cutting between his thick dark brows, 'I will make representations in the proper quarters as soon as I am able, for there will be war if I am not mistaken. Stoneyathe does not know these people. They will fight, as they have always fought, for the whole history of this country is the tale of battles to defend it against invaders. And that some of the invaders are themselves Welsh born, fattening themselves on their own countrymen, will only make hot blood boil hotter. Stoneyathe had best look to himself, for if he will not wait the judgement of the courts, then neither will the likes of Gwilym the Stone, with their families on the highway and their children starving.'

So now, from the saddle where his dark figure sat tall and easy, he replied to Nimue's overly polite words in a brusque tone.

'I thank you, no, it is enough for me that you are safely home.'

And even as she began to frame another sentence of conventional thanks and leave-taking, Pendragon ignored her, turned his horse's head and disappeared without further ado into the trees, leaving the group in the yard standing staring after him with their mouths agape.

'That man is a barbarian, a clod,' said Mary loudly. 'What manners.'

'At least he seems to have exerted himself enough to escort her home and speak a few words, however inept. That is more than any woman has ever got from him in the past,' Dorabella observed with a barely concealed sneer in her voice.

Nimue was suddenly very conscious, from their attitudes and the tones of their voices, that the sudden departure of herself and Pendragon from the festivities had indeed provoked the storm of gossip that she had envisaged, and that most of it had been scurrilous. Though she had half-expected it, she was not prepared for the avid looks of the women and the hot lust that was stirring in the torchlight in Gilbert's eyes, even though Dorabella was standing beside him. Nimue held her head proudly, trying to contain the disgust and outrage that rose within her. She longed to throw it in their faces, the fact that things were not as they imagined, that Pendragon had not touched her casually, but had honoured her instead by making her his lady and his wife.

It was sparkling with frost in the yard, and Nimue moved to the door in the wake of the ladies, Dorabella in her heavy brown velvet skirts and simple bodice, her only ornament her rosary and a long pomander chain hanging from her narrow white neck. Mary's favourite blue satin farthingale was sweeping the whole width of the inner hall. Nimue pulled her cloak more tightly about her as she passed Gilbert and stepped into the warmth of the house.

'What power she must have over men,' Dorabella's thin voice insinuated as the great door was shut behind them. Then, so quietly that Nimue hardly heard the words, dripping with the lewd suggestiveness of the overly pious, she added: 'Or perhaps it is just the same power any woman has over any man when once she has slept in his bed.'

Mary tittered, and Nimue halted at the foot of the stairs, her face going white, but Gilbert, who did not appear to have caught Dorabella's spiteful remark, had his own news to impart.

'This has been an eventful Yuletide, Nimue, for since you have been gone Grannah has gained itself a mistress. Dorabella has done me the honour to consent to marry me.'

He spoke challengingly, for he had been unwillingly enslaved by her wild behaviour the previous day, her flouting of convention – not to mention the fact that she seemed to have been conducting some sort of liaison behind his back with a man who might well pose a threat to the smooth running of his plans, and whose very appearance bespoke trouble. Moreover, Nimue had returned with a shining radiance about her that roused both his envious jealousy and a kind of low, bestial fury towards Pendragon, who had no doubt been responsible for it.

But even in the face of such prickling stabs of hostility from all sides the young woman managed to hold her temper and her poise, though she wanted nothing more than to leave them all and go to seek the solitude of her chamber, where she might be alone. She said evenly: 'I must congratulate you, then, Gilbert. And of course, Dorabella. I did not even know she was expected.'

'I was not expected. I came to bring Gilbert my Christmas box,' Dorabella said just as evenly.

'She knows how I love the music of this country, so she composed a song for me,' Gilbert said, and was unable to conceal the flattered vanity Dorabella's action had provoked within him. 'She gave us all the pleasure of hearing it.'

'Indeed?' Nimue raised polite brows. She could imagine only too well how Dorabella, who had had years of practice in enchanting cousin David with her singing, had used the occasion and her musical skills, her long pale fingers on the Celtic harp, to elicit a proposal from Gilbert. But before she could say more, Mary suddenly cut across the scene, speaking loudly from where she stood within the parlour. Her voice was high and defiant.

'That is not all, Nimue. I am to be married too.'

There was a startled silence. They all turned, and as Mary stood with her head jerked up, two spots of red burning in her cheeks, Gilbert voiced what they were all thinking.

'Mister Smith has asked you, Mary?'

At the frank disbelief in his face, his sister coloured unbecomingly, twisting her lace kerchief in her fingers. 'Yes,' she said. 'Yes, he - .' Then: ' – I – I – don't know,' and she stopped, staring at them.

Then suddenly she gave a choked sob, and ran past them all, up the stairs, pushing unceremoniously past Nimue so that the young woman staggered against the wall. As she regained her balance, she heard Dorabella murmur into the empty air, complacency in her tone:

'Now, that is strange indeed. How is it possible to mistake a proposal of marriage? I am quite certain that Gilbert has asked me.'

Nimue attended as efficiently as she could to the formalities of her home-coming, enquiring after the affairs of the kitchen and instructing Morfydd and the maids, making sure that her pony, Cariad, had been properly cared for. The man who had charge of it looked at her curiously when she went to the stables with a lantern. The beast had been ridden hard, as though it had carried its young mistress a long journey not just the miles from Pendragon, but at the look in Nimue's green eyes the man thought better than to mention it, and held his tongue.

Nimue hardly noticed his appraising stare. Her thoughts were like a torrent, carrying her along. So Dorabella had won. It was obvious that she had been skilfully playing her hand ever since Gilbert and Mary had arrived at Grannah, and Nimue privately considered she had recovered remarkably well from the frustration she must have endured at the demise of cousin David and the loss of her hopes in that direction. Well, she had Gilbert now, and Grannah with him, and it was no more than Nimue had anticipated, though it had happened all of a sudden.

Though no less suddenly than her own change in circumstances. Warmth tingling through her, Nimue tried hard to recollect exactly what Pendragon had said to her when he had mentioned marriage yesterday, but her mind was a strange blank on the subject. Had he asked her, in so many words, to marry him? Her lips curving into a little secretive smile, she thought privately that she could understand Mary's confusion, to a certain extent.

Reaching the seclusion of her chamber at last, Nimue watched as old Sion rekindled the fire, and his grand-daughter Sioned, a little rabbit of a girl with pale blue eyes and buck teeth, warmed the bed with coals in the brass warming pan. It was by now very late and she was dizzy with exhaustion, and wanted nothing more than to collapse between the linen sheets and sleep away the glories and surprises of this most eventful of days. But no sooner had Sion and Sioned left her than Mary entered and sat sulkily down on the dark oak chest at the foot of the bed. She looked like a cornered little vixen, so far as that was possible, for her hair was delicate in pale blond curls around her finely sculptured face, and a great star sapphire glowed on the whiteness of her breast, where her breath came and went very quickly.

'What magic did you work on that man?' she demanded in a low, intense voice. 'Oh, work the same for me, Nimue, I will do anything so you get Mister Smith to marry me.'

Nimue felt her heart tighten. She must step very carefully.

'He did not ask you, then?' Though there was no need, really, for the question.

Mary's eyes flashed with venom.

'He would have asked me,' she declared. 'Save that *she* came and would sing her song for Gilbert, and we must all listen. And then Gilbert spoke and there was no chance.' She drew a heaving breath. 'Oh, I can see it all now. She is a viper, and I have nursed her to my bosom. She and her foolish songs.' She paused and looked up with narrowed eyes. 'But perhaps she was not so foolish, though. She sang in that barbarous Welsh and I could not understand it, not could Gilbert, but I saw Mister Smith frown, and Mistress Emma went very red about the face. They did not like it. And as soon as they could afterwards, they went away. But he *would* have asked me, I know he would.'

'Then he will surely ask you next time you meet, Mary,' Nimue said, trying to sound reasonable and reassuring.

Mary looked up, her great cornflower eyes blank. She was picking at her kerchief with her nails, tearing it to shreds.

'But when will that be?' she demanded in a low wail. 'Dorabella and Gilbert will be married and then she will take my place here and oust me. Gilbert is such a fool. He was a fool over you, and now he is a fool over her, but at least - .' She drew a gulping breath. 'At least you do not threaten me. Oh, you must help me, Nimue. I will pay you whatever you ask. You can have my black pearls and my gold chatelaine, I do not care, but I must have him.'

'It is not a question of payment,' Nimue said sharply. She was very tired now, and she did not like the wild look on Mary's face nor the rising inflection in her voice. 'Not I nor anyone can make Mister Smith marry you. Only love will do that, if you hold to the love you have for him, and he for you.'

'Oh, love, love,' Mary hissed scornfully, dismissing it. She leaned forward. 'You are a witch, I know you are, you can work dark magic, you can give me power over him. What did you do to that terrible man with the scars? I do not care, I will do it too, Nimue, whatever it is. I have heard what they say at the Court, those who have consulted other witches. I will drink whatever you bid me, however terrible the draught, I will strip naked and give my body to the devil, and worship - .'

'Mary!' Nimue exclaimed, shock searing her to the soul. She felt sickened by the girl's low, feverish words and the glitter in her eyes.

'I am willing. I will do anything, anything, but get him for me,' Mary pleaded, very low.

There was a long silence in the chamber, while the flames crackled in the hearth. Nimue felt revulsion rise like bile in her throat, but she tried to speak calmly.

'You are mistaken, Mary. I am not a witch, and even if I were, I would not deal in magic of the sort you mean. They are leeches who would prey on you, those who tell you such things. My father was an astrologer and a wise man, yes, and he taught me how to use the powers I was given, but wisdom comes from holding fast always to love and trust and compassion – and to common sense.' She could see that Mary did not believe her, and she shrugged, making a gesture of helplessness. 'I have worked no spells such as you speak of on Mister Pendragon, and I can work none on Mister Smith. I would not if I could, for the dark brings to it only more dark. You are distraught, you do not know what you are saying. You need to rest.'

Another silence, then Mary's wide eyes, nakedly blind in their need, snapped into focus and became opaque. Nimue saw, in a flash of intuitive understanding, that the other woman would never forgive her for witnessing her need, her painful pleading, the revelation of the degrading depths to which she had been – and probably still was – prepared to descend.

'Yes, you are no doubt right, I am indeed very weary,' Mary said, yawning elaborately, her small hand over her mouth to stifle the yawn. She rose from the chest and moved to the door. 'We will forget what foolishness we have said tonight, both of us.'

It was a convincing pretence, but Nimue was not deceived. After Mary had gone, she stood for a moment irresolute, conscious that the other woman would never forgive her for what had passed between them in those few moments. She had made an enemy for life.

10

In the days that followed, it seemed as though all at Grannah kept their distance and their own counsel, so that although on the surface the household affairs proceeded as they had always done, there was a sense of waiting, of uneasy expectancy. It was as though a spark had been laid to a powder-keg, and when the powder caught, violence would rip their lives apart.

The maids and men went about their business, their voices and their solid presence reassuring to Nimue. They, at least, did not brood and watch her from beneath taut brows, as Gilbert did. She knew he wondered about her day – and even more desperately, her night – with Pendragon, and that although he was now betrothed to Dorabella, he found, as he always would, that his desires were stirred elsewhere for strength unexpectedly revealed which he longed to master, or struggle until it should master him.

She did not fear for herself, but she was very conscious now that Grannah and its occupants had taken on a phantom-like appearance in her life, hardly real, while the fierce focus of her existence was directed always to the lonely tower which was now her home, and the man who went about his daily business there, linked to her until death by their solemn pledges of love. She felt herself changing, as though she was passing through a time of testing, of refining, so that she might emerge tempered from the dark days of uncertainty with new awareness.

Gilbert spent long hours closeted in his study, frowning to himself over his papers and consulting his maps and charts and the documents of the estate. Mary, who had been unusually silent since she had gone from Nimue's chamber on the night of the young woman's return, applied herself to her needle-work, sitting as close to the fire as she dared without setting herself alight, her skirts kilted up so that her neat ankles and little feet were visible in their slippers that old Sion – who had a weak spot for her, though he would have growled a protest and spat unceremoniously if accused of such a thing – had fashioned out of skins, lined with softest wool.

Mary too was changing. There were secrets in her eyes now, and Nimue, who was accustomed to subtleties, sensed that, having been jolted by circumstances into revealing her willingness to evoke the dark powers to achieve her desires – even though fearfully and with little idea of what she was doing – Mary had tasted the heady draught of power and evil, and found, as many of the most unlikely people before her, that it fascinated her. Mary, Nimue thought, might prove to be more dangerous than her brother, and at least Dorabella's spitefulness and bigotry was open for all to witness.

And so the weeks passed, the long nights and slowly increasing days filled with the demands of the household and the beasts, as Grannah, like many another great estate, presented its solid walls foursquare to protect those within them against whatever winter and the elements might offer. The year turned. Nimue sat on the last night of December, warm in her furs, with her moonstone ring on her finger and the image of her husband held close to her heart.

The past, even that autumn journey with Gilbert and Mary from London, was indeed part of another time, and a new life was dawning now with the hesitant light of the new day, the first day of the year. Whatever it held, whatever waited for her in the future, she would never again watch alone, a girl longing for the love that would make her complete, the other half of herself. He was only a few miles distant, and she seemed to see him in her mind sitting in his chamber in Pendragon tower, thinking of her, with her little cross of iron horseshoe nails in his hands. She smiled, wishing him well across the dark night that separated them.

For herself, she had concentrated her attention since her return on her business about the place, keeping Gilbert and Mary at a distance and setting herself discreetly, but un-mistakably, apart from them. Things had been said by both of them which could not be wiped out, and she was more conscious than ever now that she was no kin to them, that they were virtual strangers in spite of their common background with life in London, and even familiarity with the Court.

In view of Gilbert's forthcoming marriage, she told him calmly that of course, she must consider her position and review her future prospects. She realised, naturally (she said with what she hoped was convincing candour), that though Mary had been glad enough to have the household concerns lifted from her shoulders, Dorabella would want to be mistress of Grannah in more than name, and might not require her services. She was quite prepared (she further declared) even to consider – perhaps – leaving Grannah.

'Leaving Grannah?' There was a pause, and she thought she saw a glimmer of sheer relief in Gilbert's eyes. Then he rallied as courtesy – however reluctantly – dictated. 'But what will you do? Where will you go?'

She knew he no longer cared, and that he found his promise to provide for her something he might well have conveniently forgotten. But in a way he had come to rely unwillingly on her capabilities and her good sense, as well as her management of the house. She thought too, with wry amusement, that he was already regretting his impetuous wooing of Dorabella in the same way he had repented of asking her father for her own hand in marriage, but this time he could not escape from the situation. Dorabella Mowas was not fatherless. And her father was not a man of dubious social standing, but a pillar of society. Moreover, Gilbert had been stirred anew by the fascination that had caught and held him on that Michaelmas day – so far away it might have been in another life – when he saw Nimue laughing on the Green. And he despised himself for it, and for his base, tormented desire to know what the scarred Pendragon was to her, and she to him.

Nimue's clear eyes revealed nothing, but Gilbert might have been aware of her insight, for he turned away as he added brusquely: 'There is always a place for you here.'

'As Dorabella's pensioner, as well as Mary's?' she said, smiling. Now that she was free – though never again to struggle alone – and now that she had a hearth of her own waiting for her to claim it, and a husband only waiting her bidding to light the candles in the tower, she could see as Gilbert could not, how wide was the world, and how there was place in it for all.

Mary was another matter. She had made no reference whatever to her conversation with Nimue concerning Mister Smith. Nor had she so much as mentioned marriage again, though the subject was very much in the air. Dorabella had returned in barely concealed triumph to Caercerrig, taking Gilbert with her so that he might formally request Jonas Mowas's permission to wed with his daughter, and the good justice's delight at an alliance between Caercerrig and Grannah resounded at once and at great speed throughout the county, carried to the ears of all as unstoppably as a forest fire.

Caercerrig was a comparatively new estate built on small enterprise, determination to learn and make the most of education and the achieving of position in society, while Grannah, for all its threadbare grandeur, carried the blood line from the princes of Gwynedd, which no eccentricity on the part of cousin David or anyone else could diminish. Jonas Mowas might not have looked kindly in a marriage between Dorabella and the ageing old man to whom she had sung in the twilight – for he was a romantic, of course – but he could take no exception to Gilbert's sophistication and manners, not to mention his comparative youth, his cultured background and his many-sided ability.

Like so many of Elizabeth's courtiers, Gilbert had learned to be a man of parts, poet, musician, gallant, as well as athlete, swordsman and conversationalist, and he could speak all the fashionable languages of the day. Jonas Mowas, who held an endearingly modest opinion of himself, felt that his daughter had won a prize indeed, and there was much to-doing afterwards in the parlour at Grannah, discussions concerning the details of the alliance and all the formalities arising from it which needed to be attended to.

Jonas Mowas and Dorabella held a supper party at Caercerrig, so that the happy pair and their prospective parent could celebrate the betrothal and toast their future. Gilbert sat constrained and tight-lipped while Dorabella glittered, snake-like, beside him, her eyes cold, pale flames, and in their places Nimue and Mary both — for remarkably similar reasons — smiled guardedly and were silent.

With the flushed encouragement of several of the local gentry, huzza-ing and clattering their wine-cups on the table, Jonas Mowas, resplendent in crimson velvet slashed with rose and peacock satin, rose from the feast to boom and bluster his way through his expressions of pleasure and his blessing on the union between Grannah and Caercerrig, so unaffectedly that the atmosphere of tension relaxed at last, and the evening proceeded in genuine accord.

'Did I not warn Stoneyathe, Dorabella will get what she sets her heart on, and by such female wiles as are incomprehensible to menfolk,' he cried, shaking a jovial head, his slavish bewilderment at his daughter's doings reverberating through his voice. He worships the girl, Nimue thought amusedly, and she terrifies him out of his wits.

Jonas Mowas lifted his goblet to further applause from his neighbours.

'The ladies, bless 'em all. Mistress Mary.' He bowed. 'You will be the next, I do not doubt, to follow down my daughter's scheming track and wheedle a husband of your own to the altar.' Then, immediately fearing he had been tactless (largely because of the cheers this aroused in his listeners, including their own ladies and daughters), he made haste, scarlet-faced, to repair the blunder. 'Though no scheming necessary, by God, for see you, we are simple folk hereabouts, and not accustomed to courtly manners and dress. So you have come among us like Gloriana herself, like Phoebe, you have descended from your car and madam, you do dazzle us.'

Awed silence greeted this unexpectedly poetic tribute, which Jonas Mowas had actually spent hours composing during the weeks since he had last viewed Mary. He possessed an irrepressibly gallant soul, and had been inspired by her delicacy of feature and small stature – for compared to the slim, sinuous height of Dorabella she was tiny indeed. The fact that she seemed to him to have an air about her of a child desirous to please, and yet somehow failing, so that there was a constant 'o' of consternation to her mouth and a bewilderment in her eyes, revealed that Jonas Mowas, alone of all his circle in the neighbourhood, was able to see the tragedy of Mary Stoneyathe, and in his clumsy, fond way, he would have alleviated what he perceived as her distress.

This evening she did indeed look well in her dark blue velvet, with her gilt hair in little tendrilled curls beneath her cap. Her cornflower eyes had acquired a new and secretive glitter since she had blurted out her passions to Nimue so disastrously, and there was something far more feline than before about her now. She was not just a pretty kitten but a devious and scheming cat who might, Nimue thought eyeing her rather warily, need more watching in her mood of withdrawal than she had ever done with her constant complaining and speaking of her mind, however tactlessly.

137

Mary had had a shock. She had revealed things about herself that perhaps even she had never suspected. And she was afraid for her security, for her home, for her future. With the eyes of the others all upon her, she responded with remarkable composure to Jonas Mowas's blandishments and lifted goblet, half-inclining her pretty head guardedly, but she said nothing. And that, Nimue thought, was in itself something to cause disquiet, for when had Mary Stoneyathe ever been able to hold her tongue?

Gereint Gwynne had spoken often about the depths to which the human spirit could descend. This, he had told those who came to consult with him, was the true business and concern of all who would achieve wisdom, not saintliness.

'The saints and the angels, they can take care for themselves,' he used to say, smiling at the slight puckers of disapproval from churchmen. 'It is on the fears of the human soul that the dark will feed and flourish, rather than on weakness or even ambition. It is fear that makes us petty – and do not mistake, we have all gone down that same road in our different ways at some time in our lives, and have to struggle to try and reach an end of it.'

Critics of his philosophy pointed out that considering fear and weakness surely diverted the mind from higher things, and Nimue herself had said the same when she was younger, particularly after she had been talking with Mary Aspinall, who desired to be a nun. Gereint had leaned back in his great chair and smiled again, but his voice was gentle as he answered her, his little wise child, struggling so seriously to find her way forward.

'Why do you think there is pain and suffering in the world, if not so that those who have managed to fight free of the devils of self-pity and the self's concern with itself, setting it above all else, can have compassion for those who still struggle, enmeshed?'

As a child, Nimue had found this concept difficult to understand but now, watching Mary, she began to see what her father had meant. The other young woman had been tempted by the possibility of dark power and the fear it evoked, to use darkness to raise her defences and prepare her armoury to seize what she wanted from life, selfish and shallow though her desires were. But however she might comprehend Mary's motives and feel sympathy for her, Nimue warned herself to be careful for herself – and never forgetting now, for Pendragon also. It would be all too easy for Mary to turn the force of her secret feelings of shame and humiliation at the revelation of her base desire, onto the person who had inadvertently witnessed them and refused, however carefully, to descend with her into the depths.

Gilbert and Mary, town creatures both, knew little of the traditions of the countryside and its customs, but especially in view of his coming nuptials, Gilbert particularly was eager to acquire the persona of the landowner of Grannah, the man whose roots were to go deep into his acres and establish himself and his own there for generations to come.

He had tolerated the familiar Yule customs, the smacking kisses between men and maids beneath the mistletoe ball, and the cheering of the ceremonial boar's head with the apple held in its mouth, dominating the Christmas feast, for he had had to learn how to play his part gracefully in such activities at Court. Misogyny and crabbiness would not have found favour with Elizabeth, who loved merriment, and her courtiers were not encouraged to be surly. So Gilbert could smile and clip the wenches as well as any other man if the occasion called for it, though he secretly despised the laughing maids with their dark Welsh faces and chattering tongues at Grannah, and the men who ogled them, fiercely amorous or bashful and red-faced, departing from the hall afterwards to the accompaniment of shrieks of mirth and familiar jesting.

There were greater, more vaulting ambitions to be achieved than storing up kisses like sweetmeats, Gilbert considered. He favoured a patriarchal, god-like attitude which would impress his household – and indeed the rest of the county – with his own importance, second to none, the undisputed lord of his house.

When he heard that cousin David had thought fit to bless his fruit trees each Twelfth Night to ensure a plentiful crop of apples – for cousin David, apparently, had considered apples essential for a staple diet and had religiously eaten the fruit each day of his life since a young man, thus, he often pointed out, ensuring the rude good health he had always enjoyed – Gilbert determined to keep up the tradition and do the same. Magnanimously (but with an eye on currying favour with the county for his openness and generosity towards his people) he decided to make an occasion of it. The whole household was enlisted to follow him in procession to the straggling orchard further up the hill, braving a bright blustery morning with white clouds chasing each other across a sky of the most brilliant rain-washed blue.

The men and maids, in holy day mood, jostled and laughed as they formed themselves into a circle about the greatest of the apple trees, paying no heed to the chill wind and the air while old Sion growled his toothless way through the words cousin David had ritually repeated every Twelfth Night to propitiate the spirits of the trees. Then to everyone's delight, the apple tree was blessed with a splash of cider from the huge bowl held ceremoniously between two of the men. One of them was a relative newcomer to the estate, the bailiff, Ralph Tollaster, a thin dark lizard of a person whose jerkin belied his status, flaunting in jewel colours instead of the homely buff and stuff of the rest of the men.

'He has ideas above his station, that one,' Nimue had told herself thoughtfully when Mister Tollaster had appeared at Grannah to commence his duties with the estate. True to form,

Gilbert had chosen an Englishman to oversee his Welsh estate workers – someone he had encountered at the butts in Chester, it appeared, a casual acquaintance merely. Like had unerringly recognised like, and they had struck up a conversation, upon which Gilbert had appointed the smooth man whose voice held the traces of the south (London, if Nimue was not mistaken) above the heads of his Welsh dependants.

Nimue was certain from the unease she felt when in his presence, that his past held secrets that were best left clouded over. And it was with growing disquiet that she noticed how he looked at her covertly as the days passed. He had not ventured to approach her, but when Christmas came, he took heart from the enthusiastic responses of the maids beneath the mistletoe ball – or at least, Nimue supposed afterwards that something of the sort was what had emboldened him. At the ceremony of the fruit trees, as all were departing in high spirits for the convivial drinking that was to follow, he made his deliberate move towards her.

'Mistress Gwynne, permit me,' his crawling voice said in her ear, as she reached to disentangle her shawl from the clutches of a briar, and his arm snaked out to jerk the fabric free. The simian face with its unpleasant sheen of sweat, in spite of the sharpness of the bright air, was uncomfortably close to her own.

'Thank you, Mister Tollaster,' she said dismissively, feigning a matriarchal aloofness beyond her years, and she would have turned and left him but that he stood in her path.

'If there is ever anything I might dare for such a beautiful woman, consider it done,' he continued, eyeing her closely, and she felt the blood rise in her cheeks.

'You are an unlikely pleader, sir,' she retorted sharply, compelled to add unfairly: 'You might be wise to keep to your station.'

He seemed unaware that the others had passed on back to the house, and only himself and Nimue were standing in the thicket, snow in piles on the dark thin trees that reached up around them. But she was very conscious of the sudden solitude, the voices merry on the other side of the hollies.

'My station?' he echoed, smiling so that her skin prickled uncomfortably. 'What is that? And what is yours, since you too are an unlikely chatelaine for Grannah, mistress. More suited to other pursuits, so I hear, like your father.'

'What do you know of my father?' Nimue demanded, whitely.

'I have acquaintances in London, who consort with wizards – and their daughters,' he stated ambiguously, and she shrank from him suddenly. It was not just his insinuations but the fact that she could see a dark cloud around him, the stain of contact with those who followed the left-hand path, arrogance and pride and even dabbling into the black arts. Such people Nimue could recognise and she always made haste to remove herself from their presence for they contaminated the very air around them.

'A lovely woman should be wedded,' he breathed, his hand seeming as though it would stray to touch her neck, and his voice took on an unpleasantly familiar tone. 'And what if she has been cast aside by such as Stoneyathe, there are others who might be aware of her particular virtues – and those possessed by her parent.'

Nimue felt the hot blood sting her cheeks at his insolent words. So he knew, as most in Wales did not, that she had been promised to Gilbert and that Gilbert had not honoured his promise to her father. Well, that had been Gilbert's failing, not hers and it was no shame to her, but she was sharply angry that this man should imagine her mind like his own, storing up wrongs, nursing resentment and bearing a grudge.

She was even more coldly angry that he should speak of Gereint Gwynne in such a crawling, suggestive manner. Gereint, who had taught her always to hold to the light. This man with knowledge of the dark around him, cloudy as dank fog. She hesitated, drawing in her breath to administer a crushing retort, one that would silence his assumptions of intimacy and free her from his boorish attentions, and as she stood irresolute, a voice spoke querulously from some distance behind her. Both of them turned.

'*Ah, cariad Duw!* Pity, pity a blind old man who has strayed from his path. In the name of charity, give me assistance, I will perish before I reach the abbey. Oh, is it anyone of goodwill that is there?'

The figure that stood beside his shaggy pony was tall and gaunt, in ragged robes stained with the yellow and orange tints Nimue recognised as marks of chemicals and preparations of metal. She had seen her father occasionally work with such things. The man's head was white, and his hair streamed down over his shoulders, rippling roughly in the wind, mingling with his long white beard, in which the metallic colours could also be seen.

He was looking directly towards Nimue and Ralph Tollaster, but his eyes were opaque, white with cataracts, so that for all their starkness, they saw nothing. There were shoes of skin tied round his feet, and a skin slung across his shoulder, along with a worn satchel. Beside him the untidy pony stood patiently, and the sky was the blue of the Virgin's robe, heart-stopping in its loveliness, beyond his bare head.

'A vagrant,' sneered Mister Tollaster contemptuously, but he moved a step from Nimue, to her relief, and after a brief pause strode away, giving her no more than a familiar, penetrating glance that made her feel besmirched before he went through the trees. 'We will speak again, lady.'

After he had gone, she felt a sense of release from an oppressive presence, and she thankfully drew in a cleansing breath of the sharp, pure air. The old man caught her attention once more, speaking again in a thin beggar's whine that increased in plaintiveness, and he struck the ground with the wooden staff he carried.

'In the name of charity, who is there? Have pity, pity the poor and the blind, who is there, in the name of all the saints, who is there, I say?'

'You are quite safe, old man,' Nimue made haste to reassure him. Though she was well accustomed to the admiration of men and usually enjoyed their attention, the bailiff's insinuations about her father, as well as his suggestiveness towards herself, had aroused in her a surprisingly strong sense of revulsion. She was glad to turn to smile at the stranger, forgetting that he could not see her.

'You have indeed gone far from your path if you seek the abbey at Basingwerk, sir. You have wandered onto the estates of Stoneyathe of Grannah.'

Then, moved to pity for his great age and the frailness of his thin frame, she went forward. 'Have you travelled far? Will you not come back with me to the house and I will give you food and good ale in the kitchen, and then you may rest awhile in the stable, you and your beast, before one of the men will put you in your way.'

But even as she watched, a strange transformation occurred. He seemed to shed years, to change from a doddering ancient to a figure of strength and power. The gaunt frail body appeared to flesh out and the seemingly ancient blind eyes took on life and fire. His tones too became mesmeric, compelling in their depths and richness, the aged pipe vanished as though she had never heard it at all.

Through her mind flashed the impossible conviction that this was the manifestation of the old wizard Pendragon. Or if not him, she amended to herself, conscious of the fact that this man was a physical being, and no spirit, then someone of the same powerfully magical breed.

'*Anawn*, your very voice is sweet as cool water, child. I told him he was bewitched, but now I see he spoke only the truth.' The words were filled with authority, and she was disconcerted by the way his shuttered eyes now seemed to pierce her face.

But she had seized on one word, and repeated it breathlessly, her heartbeat quickening.

'He?'

'Oh, indeed, who else but your bridegroom, your spelled wizard, your adoring worshipper. What fools these mortals be,' said the voice like a deep-toned bell, rich with secret amusement. 'Ah, but such is the power of love. I am your most humble servant, Mistress Pendragon. Owain ab Owain ab Yvaine, seventh son of a seventh child, for though Yvaine was but a maid, the powers were granted as potently even so.'

Nimue's hand clenched.

'Someone will hear,' she said, but he shook his head decisively.

'They are all gone. I see with other eyes, and we are quite alone. But I am no poor vagrant seeking the abbey, child. It is to find you that I have jolted my old bones on the road.' But even as he spoke, the laughter in his face mocked at the words. She thought that though he was indeed old in years, yet he had the youth of Morfydd's Llew, and the strength of Pendragon himself.

'Your husband has sent me to take you home,' he said, and the words were like balm to Nimue's soul. Her heart filled with lightness, and she questioned eagerly:

'Sir, how is my lord?'

Owain ab Owain gave a brief, tolerant shrug. There was amusement in the whole of his bearing.

'As to that, child, he is as you are yourself. Turning one moment pale, the next ruddy, falling to silences, and then into long discourses on your beauty. He is not the man he was, that is certain, though he may be twice the man he was now that he is wedded. In a word, he is a lover. In another, a husband. Combine the two of them and you have a creature who is star-crossed and fit for nothing.'

She laughed delightedly, and replied with spirit.

'You are a philosopher, sir. Yet you are a cynic also. My father used to say that love was the greatest alchemist of all.'

145

'Indeed, that is so, child,' Owain acknowledged. 'But the path of bewitchment, ah, that is perilous to tread, whatever the spell or the alchemy.' His tone altered, became brisker.

'Your husband sends his loving obediences to you, bidding you join him if you will, since he cannot sleep nor eat through pining for your sweet face and he fears he might die of love-longing in the very tower where you alone can work his recovery with your presence. In a word, Mistress Pendragon - ,' and his face creased up suddenly with ironical amusement, ' - he is very well and manages to satisfy his manservant by clearing the board each time he sits down to meat, and indeed, snores like one in a deep sleep throughout the night, for I have heard him myself, and so do not fret you over his pleading. Like all men in love, he is selfishness personified and you must needs ignore his plaints if you would live to love him in old age, or else the thought of his sufferings will drive you into your own early grave.'

Nimue found herself laughing all the more, joy bubbling up within her.

'He does not care then, he does not think of me?'

'Indeed, he composes sonnets by the hour to your beauty, and declaims them to the air, bidding the birds fly to you and sing them at your chamber window,' Owain assured her, straight-faced. 'Save that the wild creatures have sense, and do not suffer as we do from the affliction of sentimentality. And so they take no heed of such foolishness, and having better things to do, they go straight about their business.'

In a different tone, he went on: 'Your husband is well, and would disdain to let me reveal how thoughts of you companion him through the day, lest you should delay in hastening to share with him the promise of the night. Will you come with me and go to him?'

Nimue looked round, shivering suddenly, once more aware of the trees silent in the bright morning, the pale winter sunlight

146

striking sparks from mounds of snow in their branches, the cold and solitude of the scene.

'I will come to him as soon as I may, but not yet,' she said, very serious. She felt she could trust this man of wisdom and humour, his very presence inspired confidence. Surely the old wizard, Pendragon's father, who had been his friend, had been such a person. She spoke now to Owain as candidly as she might have spoken to the old wizard himself.

'I love him with all my heart, and I long for nothing else but to be with him. And I have spoken with Gilbert, that I will leave Grannah soon, but for my dear lord's sake, I cannot go to him yet. Gilbert will provoke violence with his mad ambition and his stupidity, he sits with secret matters closeted in his chamber, at any moment a spark may strike, and I would warn my husband. And Mary - .'

She hesitated. The wise eyes sharpened.

'Yes?' Owain said gently.

'I do not know - . She will have Mister Smith, and she is desperate. She is willing to sell her soul for him, I think.'

Nimue revealed no more, but she felt that Owain understood everything, even that he was aware of what had been said on her return to Grannah, when Mary had pleaded for her to invoke the dark powers.

'She could be dangerous,' the young woman added slowly. 'More dangerous even than her brother, perhaps.'

Owain regarded her gravely.

'You wish me to tell your husband you will remain?'

'I will not go yet, until – until we know what they plan, what they might do,' Nimue said reluctantly, and he smiled with such warmth that she felt flooded with strength and courage.

'Bide then,' he told her quietly. 'And I will tell him you will come to him soon.'

'As soon as I may. I long to be with him,' she admitted, then, shivering again in the crisp air, she invited: 'Will you not come with me to the house and take some refreshment after your ride, sir?'

'I will return, for I too have work to do,' he told her. 'I have not yet fulfilled the task for which your husband summoned me.'

'He has told you? You have seen it – the stone?' she ventured hesitantly, and he smiled.

'I have seen it, and the writings concerned with it. But there is yet snow lying on that part of the mountain, and I cannot prospect to discover it.'

Nimue looked into his strange, shuttered, yet powerful face and though she was sure he could not see, he appeared to sense her gaze and meet it inscrutably.

'Do you think there is gold to be found, sir?' she dared to ask, and added, troubled: 'I have seen what gold can do to men.'

There was a silence, then:

'To whom, then, would you assign the task of judging the earth's bounty, if not each for himself? Would you deny yourself water, calling it evil because, unrestrained, it has the power to drown you?' Owain said, shifting his weight, leaning against his shaggy pony which patiently moved, seeming used to the habits of its master.

'Oh, yes,' he went on, 'there is gold somewhere to be found on Pendragon land. A good heritage, if it is handled wisely. A gift of love, to regard in the spirit of the giver. The information is clear, it was recorded by your husband's father in his own hand, that I knew well. Yet, though he desired his son to have the gold, there are many considerations to such a matter.' He thought for a moment, then spoke softly, his manner becoming absent.

'I know well these mountains, I am as familiar with the rocks as my own self. I know them and can read them. If the gold is there, it is in old workings long since abandoned, perhaps where the copper ran out. So the record stands. But gold is elusive, child. There may be a rich vein, indeed, it would seem so, yet a rich vein of such gold as I saw in your husband's rock sample is rare, though tradition will linger always, for gold indeed has magical allure. The workers who took the copper – or the lead – from their workings must have known of it, as my old friend Pendragon knew of it, and yet this knowledge he has imparted was a private thing, and there is no general tradition of gold on Pendragon land. The lode perhaps is too small, perhaps it cannot be worked.'

'Gold is gold, surely,' Nimue said wonderingly. 'How could it not be worked, if it is there?'

'Out of ignorance you speak, child,' Owain told her. 'The working of metal is a lifetime's apprenticeship. But do not fret, child. If it can be done, you shall have your gold. I must speculate only, until I can find it.'

Nimue said suddenly, as though something prompted her:

'Tell Pendragon, Gilbert has asked Dorabella Mowas to marry him, and they will be wedded in June, Jonas Mowas is inviting the county. Dorabella rules Gilbert now, even though through constraint and not love. And Ralph Tollaster, his bailiff, is his toady, and I think will do his left-hand bidding. He is from London and also serves his ambition, and he would - .' Colour surged up into her cheeks. 'He knows of my father, and that Gilbert would not wed me, and he would have me, if he could. He has the dark all about him, but I believe that I can call on stronger powers, and I have no fear for myself. I am anxious only what he – or Gilbert – or any of them – might intend towards Pendragon tower. Tell my dear lord, and assure him I will come to him soon. And now, if you do not return with me, sir, I will give you good-day, or I will be missed.'

And then, before she could weaken and tell Owain that she would leave at that very moment to go with him to her husband with never a backward look, she turned and ran through the fruit trees with their thin bare branches, to the house.

11

It was too much, she thought, half-rueful, half-amused, to hope that Gilbert might change, acquire maturity and moderate his ambition and greed. But the more she considered the matter in the days that followed, as January passed in dark wind and sleet that melted the snow into morasses, splashing the ponies to their bellies and streaming down the hill, through the yard, and even in wet pools forming everywhere within the house itself, the more she began to feel reassured that Pendragon was right. There was nothing to fear.

For all his capacity to initiate the sort of rivalries and feuds that split many a pate when the servants of one house clashed with another, which happened often in Wales and with particular vigour in Flintshire at that time, Gilbert was no real threat but only an irritant, like a buzzing fly in high summer. And her husband was not a child. He could easily swat away any nuisance that might be directed against Pendragon.

Nimue began to realise, with mingled sheepishness and pride, that she had, in an excess of impetuous devotion, grossly underestimated the power of her new lord. She suspected that he had simply been indulging her need to feel she was able to protect him, when he let her return alone to Grannah to play the spy. She had a growing certainty that he was more than able to protect himself, with no help from her or from anyone else.

Yet his care for her pride, his understanding – sensitively unexpressed – warmed her through. This was the true strength of which her father had spoken, the power that did not need to assert itself. He would wait until she went to him at the time of her own choosing, having discharged the responsibilities she had undertaken, when she felt satisfied she could leave the past – and the present – safely behind and accept joyfully the future they would share. He had understood better than she had herself that she needed just a little time, time to catch her breath, to gain her balance.

But all the same, she knew that she was free of Grannah now, and that Gilbert and Mary knew it also. She had passed beyond Stoneyathe, and though she did not think she would be any better able to act than her husband in Pendragon tower if the need for action should arise, she was still for the moment a part of the world outside Pendragon walls, a part of society with its eternal gossip and rumour, its familiar patterns of universal life that rose and fell, greed, pettiness, ambition, desire, suffering and injustice. And it was not from Gilbert's machinations but from a wider unrest which seethed beneath the surface of this society that trouble, if it came, might emerge to threaten them.

It had been smouldering further afield than Stoneyathe property, beyond Flint and Chester, beyond Denbigh to the west. It was everywhere, gathering force, muttered beneath men's breath, in their curses and the cries of the women and children who starved and shivered in the grip of the bitter nights and long dark days.

More than ever, Nimue was aware of the fact that she lived in times of change. It had always been the lord, the landowner, to whom people turned. And the lord, the rich man in his castle, had accepted the responsibility for his people, honouring traditions of blood and breeding, of communal caring for those of his lineage who could also trace their ancestry back to the same shadowy ghosts which stalked the mountains and the woods of this ancient land. The ties of race were eternally binding in Wales.

But now, suddenly – and not only at Grannah – smooth-talking officials of the like of Ralph Tollaster, mounted on their well-fed horses, thickly cloaked against the weather, were knocking on the walls of small cottages and hovels not to enquire into the well-being of tenants, but to demand new rents that could not be paid. Crying children and sick women stood in the snow, or trudged the highways carrying their bundles hopelessly on their backs. Gilbert's men were not the only ones who enforced new boundaries and appropriated pasture and grazing, tiny plots where common livings had been scraped, with brutal indifference, and dealt callously with those who tried to argue.

The blame, in the minds of the poor, lay with all who held land, whether they favoured enclosure or not. Popular feeling ran blindly against the sheer injustice perceived as perpetrated by general misuse of power by those who had – especially because some of these were upstarts, new men who had come from nowhere – against those who had nothing. Simmering unrest could break like a wave, too long held back, and then all, whether they were guilty or not, would be swamped if they were in its path.

Nimue, along with the rest, heard tales of violence, of local people desperate, men who were taking matters into their own hands with increasingly impotent fury, their own survival and that of their animals, which would ensure food and a roof over the heads of their families, denied them. The wrath that Gilbert and his like aroused in those who were victimised by them was not rational, and might turn itself mindlessly against any great house without discrimination. Even against Pendragon.

It did not help matters either, Nimue thought reluctantly, but trying not to turn from the reality of the situation, that in the eyes of the foolish and the ignorant, those people who were set apart, different, who had always dwelt in Pendragon's crumbling tower were suspected of meddling in the blackest and most terrible of magic, and so whenever the occasion called for it, they were likely to be conveniently blamed for everything. They were scapegoats, to be sacrificed in place of those real oppressors who were untouchable.

With a chill at her heart, she found herself remembering the young swan-necked woman at Southwark, stumbling clumsily with her child, while the little boy, dark-faced, shielded his cat as best he could while he tried to stand between his mother and the mob – the jagged blood-lust, the panic, the crimson-splashed flowering of fear.

Her own position at Grannah had changed too, even though Gilbert and Mary might be unaware just how drastically, and she was uneasily conscious of personal vulnerability. Though Gilbert had not dared to question her about her acquaintanceship with a man who was notorious throughout the county, and whom she had – so far as he knew – never met, her visit to Pendragon at Christmas had been a stark reminder to him and to Mary that she had a separate existence, that she was not, if indeed she had ever been, one of them.

Gilbert's hot secret lust had been aroused, Mary's enmity and suspicion. She was not only the daughter of a wizard with sinister powers, it seemed, she had been exposed in her true colours as the very opposite of the sweet maiden all had assumed because of her brightness and the clarity of her eyes. A temptation to Gilbert, a threat to Mary and Dorabella and all the decent folk who were attempting to live pious, well-ordered lives. She was a low and brazen hussy whose amorous affairs were probably legion, and who had who knew what sort of dark experience of men. That thought tormented everyone, to a different degree.

Nimue would never regret her decision to go to Pendragon. She knew her life would be empty indeed without him, but she was increasingly glad she had not revealed that she and Pendragon were wedded. Gilbert's dark fascination and fancy was volatile, he would take the matter as a personal insult, for though he had not been willing to marry her himself, he could not bear the thought that someone else might have her.

She sighed. It would always be thus with Gilbert. But if his jealousy and vanity were touched on the raw, who knew what he might not do, especially when the woman who might have saved him was flawed. Dorabella had no respect for him nor love.

Nimue had come to realise, as she watched the other young woman at the harp, singing to Gilbert, or riding out with him to hawk or practise her archery at the butts, or looking into his eyes as they toasted each other with wine in Grannah's silver cups that Nimue had spent hours polishing to a fine sheen, that Dorabella despised men. Even Jonas Mowas's fond, well-meaning, blustering indulgence of his daughter had only increased her cold contempt for all the male sex.

When she heard that Nimue had spoken of leaving Grannah, Dorabella had cast a thoughtful glance towards the young woman's bent head as Nimue sat sewing on the other side of the fire, her needle flashing in and out of her work. Apropos of nothing, she remarked idly that she was sure Madam Gwynne would have no trouble at all in finding a more congenial place for herself in some other house – in fact, her father would probably know of someone who would be please to take her in. Her silence and doggedness would, Dorabella was sure, be ideally suited to the caring of some aged, sick person, one whose uncertain temper would reduce less phlegmatic attendants to tears.

She elaborated with satisfaction for some moments on the picture of a sort of elderly dame with flat, dull features and uninspired conversation, doomed to the disagreeable existence of housekeeper-maid and body servant, choosing to ignore the fact that in her green gown, Madam Gwynne was looking as fresh and young as a spring morning.

'A gentleman who suffers from the gout, perhaps,' Dorabella murmured cruelly. 'Oh, it would be a tragedy indeed if the strange talents that she has are not given the fullest employment. Unless - .' And she paused, catching her lip between her sharp little teeth as though overcome by inspiration. 'She might of course marry. Oh, I mean, within her own station, where she would be comfortable. With your generous remembrance of her service here, Gilbert, she will make quite a catch for some hard-working man of the steward sort.' Speculatively, 'I believe Mister Tollaster would have her, indeed, and then - .' She gave a little tinkling laugh that had no mirth in it, ' – why, then Grannah would not have to lose her.'

Nimue's head came up with a jerk. She had little patience with Dorabella's childish spitefulness, and would have said so scornfully, but that there seemed to be restraining hands on her shoulders. She felt as though her father was gentling her as he might have calmed a nervous horse. And after a moment, her sense of humour came to her rescue.

'Thank you for your concern of me, Dorabella,' she said sweetly. 'But I could never think of marrying with Mister Tollaster. I fear I would not be able to conduct myself in the manner that would be befitting to the wife of such a man. I am well aware of my station. Some ancient gentleman with the gout sounds far more likely, or I have even considered retreating within the walls of a nunnery and withdrawing altogether from this sad, cruel world. I am sure I would be welcome even without a dowry, as I am so skilled at scrubbing and washing and domestic labour, and I would be able to make myself very useful to the community in a humble sort of capacity.'

This speech was met with silence, Dorabella frowning as she wondered whether Nimue was making mock of her. After that, she said no more, and Ralph Tollaster, who had undoubtedly been informed of Nimue's words, also made no move to approach her again, though she was conscious of his curiously yellow eyes upon her, causing her just as consciously to seek the cleansing power of her crystal and her thoughts, alone in her chamber.

On a bright, fine morning in late January, she was debating with a rising sense of liberation how best to put it to Gilbert that she was leaving Grannah. Once she had gone, it would be time enough to think about what his reaction would be – the reaction of the whole country, in fact – when it was revealed that she was Mistress Pendragon, that the sinister misogynist of Pendragon tower had been outwitted by a woman at last.

Her lips curved into a mischievous smile at the thought, and her eyes sparkled. One more episode to be entered in the local store of well-thumbed tales to be repeated at firesides on dark winter evenings. She and her husband were already assuming the stature of legendary beings because of their Christmas flight from the festive board at Grannah. How much more the maids would widen their eyes – and their minds – at the news that they had been clandestinely married.

With a lightness of heart, Nimue went out into the fresh morning to collect the eggs – a duty that was not that of the housekeeper, far less the chatelaine of an establishment like Grannah, but Nimue did not believe that an elevated position precluded the undertaking of simple tasks if the occasion called for it, and she relished the sharpness of the air after the heat of the kitchen. It would clear her head and enable her better to form her plans.

But while she was searching in the straw in a dark corner of the stable, with her basket over her arm and one of the eggs in her hand, she paused, stiffening as she heard Gilbert's voice. There were two words that penetrated her preoccupation with her own eager thoughts and brought her up as sharply as if he had drenched her with icy water.

'Pendragon' and 'gold'.

She waited, scarcely breathing, and heard sounds of the movement of a horse, and then Ralph Tollaster's voice in reply.

'I have it on good authority, Mister Stoneyathe. There is gold on the mountain.'

'Why do you tell me this, Ralph?' Gilbert demanded suspiciously, for in his mind such knowledge was not to be shared but to be kept secret and acted on privately, lest others should benefit.

'There are those who, like myself, have reason to want to see the old order overturned – we can visualise the future in the

156

hands of those who are marked for leadership, for high station, not just because their name is old and they have lived for centuries in some ancient tower.'

He was a fawning lick-spittle, Nimue thought with angry contempt, sensing rather than seeing how Gilbert stirred sleekly beneath the words like an animal that has been cunningly stroked.

'Who are these people?' he demanded, and she sensed a slight movement denoting a shrug.

'Best if you do not know, master. Then nothing can be proved to have had your compliance.'

There was a silence. Nimue's heart was beating so loudly that she felt panic in case the men might hear the unsteady beats. Then Gilbert's voice again, elaborately casual.

'You are right, Ralph. This man Merlin Pendragon, for instance, I doubt we will ever be able to agree on certain matters, though he is wrong and I am in the right. But however much I might desire him to be brought to see reason - .' The seconds lengthened almost unbearably, then Gilbert went on: 'I could never of course condone violence, for instance.'

In the explosively still pause that followed, Nimue realised with a sort of mist beginning to blur her eyes, just how far Gilbert was prepared to go to have what he wanted. He and Mary were indeed two from the same stable. She strained her ears feverishly as he spoke again.

'This matter of gold - .'

'Pendragon has been seen on the mountain with an old reprobate like his father, a Druid, they say. He is called Owain ab Owain, a miner from Halkyn, whose business is the working of metals,' said Ralph Tollaster, and Nimue felt her skin crawl with horror to hear their secrets so casually thrown to Gilbert, to make what he would of them.

'Does that signify gold?' Gilbert's voice was thick, hoarse with anticipation.

'Metal, certainly. He has spent his life in the earth and knows no other love, they tell me. But as for gold - .'

Nimue waited, every muscle tense. Who had betrayed Pendragon, betrayed herself and all who dwelt in Pendragon tower? Not Huw, she would have sworn, she would have staked her life on it. Math, then? The boy was young, and for all the instinctive light and wisdom in his eyes, perhaps he had been tempted and been too weak to resist.

'One of them entered the tower,' Ralph Tollaster said in a colourless voice. Her blood began to seethe, that someone had actually dared, had trespassed in that place of magic and peace where the globe of the stars gleamed softly in the candlelight. 'Oh, not one of the men. His woman, who is powerful in her own right and who is familiar with the signs and secret instruments of sorcery, undertook to venture in - .'

Nimue could almost see the lizard-like smile stretching his lips.

' - For a price, of course. I thought it good. He will challenge you in law, over the fences, but he is a wizard after all, and are not wizards anathema to the church and to society? With proofs of his sorcery, you can accuse him openly and have a clear way - .'

But while Nimue listened, as a stoat will stand paralysed before a snake, waiting helplessly for it to strike, there was an interruption. One of the maids came out into the yard, carrying a pail and laughing, calling over her shoulder. Gilbert hissed quickly to Ralph Tollaster.

'Enough. Go on your business now. We will speak more. The gold, though? What of the gold?'

'She saw a little chest, that contained a rock – and she brought the rock out of the tower with her. It is gold bearing, unmistakable, visible, a rich vein. They must have been looking for the lode, prospecting the place where it is to be found.'

Even as Ralph Tollaster mounted his horse, and there were sounds of harness and hooves, Nimue almost saw how Gilbert seized him by the arm, and would not allow him to go.

'Where is this rock?'

There was another pause. Nimue sensed that the bailiff was smiling.

'I have it safely, you need have no fear, Mister Stoneyathe,' he said, with triumph underlying the humble note of his voice. And then he was gone, and Gilbert was standing alone in the yard.

As soon as he had disappeared, Nimue fled to the safety of the kitchen, where she saw to the preparation of the food without awareness of the utensils she was handling, or paying any thought to the pastry her fingers kneaded. Trying to keep calm, she debated what she should do.

But now that she was free of Gilbert's tense presence and the undermining of Tollaster's insinuating voice, homely household tasks and reflection calmed her somewhat. Pendragon and Owain must surely be aware that the rock had gone. They might even know who had taken it. And until they had found the place where the gold was, then Gilbert would take no action. Even he, for all his greed, would not be so foolish as to attack or injure the only two people who knew the secret of that golden-veined stone. And somehow, she was increasingly sure that the papers relating to the source of the gold had not been consulted. Perhaps the woman had not realised what they were.

It would not help matters if she ran from Grannah. Better to stay and watch, spy and listen.

When the household had retired Nimue sat in her chamber with the crystal before her and sought further enlightenment. She let her mind dwell on the woman who had entered Pendragon – someone who, Ralph Tollaster had said, possessed the powers. Who was she? And just how powerful was her power?

The answer came easily. She saw only lust for power, lust for stirring up fear and using it. The woman, whoever she was, had no real vision, and had forfeited what she had been given through her pettiness and greed. Thankfully, Nimue dismissed her, but the attention Gilbert and Ralph Tollaster were now turning towards Pendragon was disturbing. She would go tomorrow and lay the matter in her husband's hands, she decided as she replaced her crystal within her father's leathern satchel and lay down to sleep.

Mary had been fretting. The weeks were passing and she had not seen Ignatius Smith.

As Nimue had suspected, Mary, frustrated by her refusal to summon the dark powers, had turned to seek out another source that would gratify her desires. As in the case of her brother, like had recognised like, and Mary had ventured, in fear and trembling, to consult Ralph Tollaster on the matter. The bailiff had relieved her of her black pearls, and in exchange put into her hands a philtre that he told her had come from a witch – one of the wild Welsh women of the hills with streaming hair and fierce falcon eyes. Mary had drunk it in nervous terror, afraid it would kill her, but reasoning that if she could not have Ignatius Smith, she might as well die anyway.

She had been very sick, but had not died, and with growing confidence now tormented herself that the lawyer would on sight be bound by magic to love her and ask her to wed with him. But since she had not seen either him nor Mistress Emma, nor indeed anything of society since Christmas except for the Mowas's and their guests at Caercerrig, he had had no chance to make her a happy woman, and her increasingly petulant moans drove Gilbert in the last week of January to despatch one of the men to Flint with an invitation requesting Mister Smith's presence at Grannah. He himself had much to discuss, and his sister would regard it as an honour if Mister Smith and Mistress Emma would attend a supper party on the night of Candlemas. She promised good cheer and good company.

160

12

It was the stirring of the spring, of new life and hope. Candlemas, the old festival of Imbolc. Nimue had celebrated this day with her father in past years, lighting her own candles in a joyous 'crown of light' to Bride and Bridget, the goddess and the saint, with no sense of difference between them. As Gereint Gwynne often pointed out when challenged on points of dogma:

'In the eye of God, one is all and all is one. Is my vision greater than that of the beasts, because I can quote Socrates or Plato? The lowly creatures trust in their maker and ask no questions, which is more than man's gift of free will and all his thinking permits him to do.'

Nimue felt an uplifting of hope, and was filled with optimism as she rose in the still dark of the morning. Perhaps, even though she could not dismiss the fact that Gilbert now knew of the gold, and that Ralph Tollaster brought trouble with him whenever he appeared, clammy-skinned and soft-footed, and Mary was working herself up into frenzy over her meeting with Mister Smith at the supper party tonight, she could still go and leave them, trusting that all would be well.

The night had brought a sense of perspective, and this morning was fresh with new beginnings. She was sorely tempted to go to Pendragon tower straight, to saddle Cariad and ride away, to leave the household to fend for itself.

When the kitchen was bustlingly astir, and she saw that the maids were at the morning's business, impulsively, she took her cloak and went through the yard and up the hill past the ancient apple tree and the orchard wall. She lifted her face to the sun, which was just rising in a sky the colour of the little wild primroses that were blowing in the new grass of meadow and wood, and found herself laughing aloud, breathless, into the wind as she climbed to the top of the hill where there was a huge and ancient rock – some said, tossed there from the hands of King Bendigeidfran – that in the winter sheltered the sheep, and in hot summer gave the coolest of shade. She stood with the cold wind stirring her hair, looking across the dark patchwork of the landscape towards the south-east, where she knew Pendragon was, and sending her thoughts and her intentions with the wind and the birds, tossing gold-bright in the high glittering air.

And then, with a strange sense of fatefulness that seemed to hold her still in a moment that was aeons long with the stopping of time, she saw him. Riding towards her across the wild coarse moor-land turf, close cropped by the eternal sheep and still splashed with patches of unmelted snow, he was mounted on his great white horse, which he called Taliesin. He was coming out of the dawn and as she looked she seemed to see the sun's rays thickening around him in a cloud, obscuring his image so that she had to blink hard. Her senses were leaping with delight and she could feel his love reaching out to her, cradling her as though he held her against him, her head pressed into the hollow of his shoulder.

Yet even as she watched, her intuition told her that he was not what he seemed. And when she blinked again the light was clear, the image of her husband was gone, the heath stretched emptily to the still-dark night-blue line of the mountains on the horizon in the west. Turning, not understanding, Nimue saw that the figure of Huw, his white robes fluttering in the wind, was standing impassively watching her. She took a faltering step towards him.

'What is it? What has happened?'

Then she remembered that Huw could not speak.

'Do you bring me word from my lord?' she asked, trying to remain composed though her body was thrilling with in-explicable alarm. He smiled, his dark face lightening reassuringly. She could feel the strength of his serenity, his

162

stillness, and she recognised for the first time his strange and ancient power of which Pendragon had spoken.

As she halted, her eyes pleading for enlightenment, Huw reached out one hand and gently touched her on the forehead. She felt peace pass from his fingers into her mind, and she shut her eyes, still not comprehending but with a certainty that all, in spite of her fears, was well. The vision of her husband had been sent in deep love, in response to her own troubled thoughts, and Huw had come in person to relieve her anxieties. She opened her eyes and saw Math also, standing a little apart, down the hill from the stone, with two ponies.

'My lord is well?' she faltered, and Huw's strange, light eyes seemed to speak for him. All, she knew then with utter certainty, was progressing as it should. Out of concern for her anxiousness and her caring, her worry whether to stay or go, Pendragon, who was not free himself to come to Grannah, had sent his emissary to bid her remain until he came. No letter, no message was necessary, for Huw's eyes and the touch of his dark hand on her brow told her everything.

She smiled, needing nothing more, and with a slight grave inclination of his head, Huw turned and went down to where Math waited. In a moment, the two were riding away from her. But Nimue still stood, watching them. Her hand was on her lips as though she would send a kiss, but knowing there was no need. Pendragon could feel her love as though she reached out to touch him. Comforted, she returned to the house and was content now to tackle her duties in kitchen and parlour, listening to Morfydd and the maids, but herself silent. She had had the burden of her awareness lifted from her. She would go when her husband came to fetch her. In the meantime, there was much to do for the proper entertainment of the evening's guests.

Gilbert and Ralph Tollaster rode out before noon, and she watched them go thoughtfully. Gilbert was displeased. His eyes were fretted into sparks of anger, in contrast to the opaqueness of the bailiff's yellow glance, which flicked familiarly across Nimue's slim form as they rode past her, making her feel as though she had been physically touched. Yet because she could fear nothing now and would not be petty, she countered his insolence composedly with a half-smile, refusing to be troubled by him.

But she wondered where they were going. And what had been said further concerning Pendragon, or the gold. There was tension in the air, she could feel it. In spite of herself, she found herself staring uneasily after them, as though Gilbert's tautly held back and the stiffness of his neck would give her answers.

But when he returned alone, he seemed in much better spirits. She saw him from the casement of the parlour, where she was beeswaxing the dark chests and presses, a sack tied round her kilted skirts. The brightness of the day had encouraged her to attack her goodwife's freshening of the house with renewed zeal and she and the maids had been strewing fresh rushes and polishing and bustling all that afternoon, in preparation for the supper that was already simmering and roasting ready for the festivities of the evening.

Nimue saw Gilbert cross the yard and disappear into the house. She was aware that there was a difference in him since the morning. The tension and anger had been replaced by a sort of white, still intensity, the turning within himself the vortex of his deepest impulses. His face had lost his usual slight, aloof frown. It was a mask, and she could not read it. But because his attentions were obviously directed elsewhere than towards anything around him, she was somewhat reassured and turned back to her beeswax and vinegar and her polishing until she could see her face in the dark wood.

Mary Stoneyathe, who had dared her everything including her soul, for her hope of Mister Smith, spent the afternoon tormenting Sioned, who was unsuccessfully attempting to play the lady's maid, into tears of blubbering desperation as the two prepared the mistress of the house for the evening. But at last, she was satisfied.

Outwardly she was flawless. Her skin glowed fair as milk, and her hair was palest silk, drawn back from her face beneath a cap of blue satin. Her slender waist was clasped with a jewelled belt that swung over the bell-like folds of her skirt, and her neck and shoulders glowed with a pearly lustre. She had never looked finer even when she had been in the presence of the Queen. But tonight, she was triumphantly ready to claim her reward for throwing down the gauntlet so recklessly to life. And when she descended at last, Nimue looked at her soft, moist mouth drawn up like a slightly petulant rose, and thought with unwilling admiration that no man would be able to resist this taut, newly passionate creature, certainly not Mister Smith, who had already been smitten by her. The whole household was aware that she had hopes of him, though not of the steps she had taken to ensure that her desires were fulfilled.

And yet, there was something else about Mary now that was difficult to define, but touched her with shadow. Something repellent. Distasteful. The willingness to allow the dark into her heart had begun to reflect itself on the purity of Mary's face and form. For all her perfection, there was rottenness at the core, and Nimue had seen before how such putrefaction made itself manifest even on the most beautiful women, the richest men, the greatest scholars and intellects.

She felt a stab of pity for Mary as she saw how the other woman waited, outwardly careless but seeming to vibrate tensely on the air, until the guests should ride into the yard. It was as though a shrill, tinny sound that could not be heard, was all about her. It was uncomfortable to be near her, and the sense of discomfort increased as the moments passed.

But at last they came, Jonas Mowas escorting Dorabella and the dowager Lady Ffirth, an old friend of the Mowas's, in her coach. Lady Ffirth's eyes in her wrinkled face were bright as a bird's in the expectation of an evening of eating too many sweetmeats and marchpane, drinking too much and most of all, having personable young men to flirt with. Goronwy Tudor and two other local gallants who made their education seductions and the pleasures of the card-room and the dice, had been bidden and arrived having raced each other on sweating horses, hallooing and waving their caps in the air. Their beasts were led away to be rubbed down and watered, old Sion shooting a venomous glare towards the retreating backs of the swaggering trio for their carelessness of blooded animals.

Mary, biting her lip viciously so that she had almost drawn blood, was still hovering at the great door of Grannah in the fading evening light when Ignatius Smith and his sister rode into the yard, Mistress Emma plumply ensconced in a swathe of cloaks and furs, but sitting her mare like the Welshwoman she was. At the sight of the lawyer Mary's face flamed scarlet and then drained to bone white, and her eyes burned blue.

She stepped forward ostensibly to greet the latest arrivals, holding out her hands to Mistress Emma and effusively kissing her on both cheeks, but hardly able to contain herself before she turned like a predator to its prey, to the stocky, sombrely-cloaked figure of the lawyer. But Mister Smith had caught sight of Lady Ffirth, with whom he had some trifling business to discuss, and he stepped towards her, ignoring Mary. When, in her explosive fury of disappointment she put one hand on his arm, grasping his sleeve and almost pulling him round to her, he turned.

There was a moment when they looked at each other, gazes locked. What Ignatius Smith could see in Mary's eyes, Nimue, who had witnessed the brief exchange, did not know but she saw him pull his arm slightly – but with unmistakable deliberation – from Mary's grasp and bow towards her with chill formality, before he turned even more deliberately back to Lady Ffirth.

It was over within the space of a single heartbeat, but something had happened, something that had robbed Mary of her prey. As Nimue watched with disquiet, she seemed to coil into herself like springing steel, though for politeness, and because she had spent years at Court learning how to dissemble, no-one but Nimue – and Ignatius Smith – was aware of it. She turned her back in turn on Mister Smith, jaw set while her eyes blazed impotently, and her knuckles, within the folds of her gown holding her fan, were white.

It was not a propitious beginning but the ill-assorted company relaxed at length into a semblance of enjoyment of the good food and drink Grannah hospitably provided. Mary, who had not spoken a word, even managed to convince herself that in the morning when the feast was over and the rest had gone, Mister Smith, who was remaining to spend the morning discussing business with Gilbert, would be more amenable when she got him alone. She could not possibly lose him, not now. She had, after all, swallowed a love philtre and had nearly died. She could not understand what had happened, and in a single-minded frustration brooded darkly while she drank deep from her cup of wine.

At length, the company was settled in the parlour, Lady Ffirth laughing loudly with Goronwy Tudor so that the paint on her face began to run, and declared she had not enjoyed herself so much in years. Dorabella ran her long fingers over the harp, and Gilbert said he had remembered some parts for a round that he had brought from Chester and excused himself to fetch them. Nimue suddenly recalled that she had not placed fresh candles in his chamber, and slipped out to do so.

She had a few words with Morfydd in the kitchen and then, not trusting any of the maids to wait on the master, she went up the stairs, carrying the new candles she had made that week, of best beeswax for Gilbert's use, in her hand.

His chamber door stood half open and she went in unthinkingly, only to stop short on the threshold as she entered. He was there, a shadow dim in the moonlight and the points of cold stars beyond the casement, dim in the dark. She saw by the light of her own taper that he was holding something in his hands, and as he looked up at her there was an expression on his face that sent a shock of alarm through her. Her eyes, of their own volition, looked down at the object he held.

It was not the paper sheets, the parts of the round. Though the taper gave only a glimmer, her inner vision was clear, and she saw that it was the rock from the oiled wooden chest at Pendragon. It gleamed subtly even as she stared, with the lovely sheen of yellow-red. She looked up again, and she and Gilbert were silent for what seemed an aeon, not breathing, their glances locked as inexorably as the antlers of two stags who must fight to the death.

Nimue felt as though her father was once again beside her physically, his hand on her arm restraining her, his fingers urgent across her mouth as she would have spoken. With a great effort she turned away, saying nothing, and managed to set the candles down carelessly on the press.

'You will need these, Gilbert.'

He eyed her with cold suspicion, but after a moment, shielding the rock with his hand, relaxed.

'Thank you.'

And them, as she turned to leave the chamber, they both heard the sounds from the yard. Clamorous barking, shouts. The clatter of horses' hooves. A scream from someone, one of the women, and voices, questioning. Deeper voices in answer. And then loud to the sky, that most terrible of cries: '*Diawl*, it is murder! Murder!'

Gilbert was still holding the rock, and as Nimue looked across at him she saw in his eyes not surprise, but guilt. Then he pushed the rock into his doublet and, moving fast on his feet, went from the chamber, pushing past her. She ran after him down the stairs, her heart beating sickeningly in terrible awareness.

Figures were emerging from the parlour, questioning, crowding into the hall. The dowager Lady Ffirth, not to miss whatever might be happening, clung determinedly to Goronwy Tudor's arm while he, drunkenly, shouted:

'What sport? What sport?'

Mary and Dorabella were both silent, their eyes hooded, and Jonas Mowas and Ignatius Smith went coolly ahead into the yard. The servants were there, clustered together, and the yard was bobbing with torches.

There were three men there, and two horses. Nimue recognised the men as labourers on the estate, one of them hardly more than a lad. Across the back of a pony he was leading, a black, inert shape lolled bonelessly, like a bundle of rags.

'What noise is this?' Gilbert shouted angrily. 'What is the cause?'

One of the men stepped forward, addressing Jonas Mowas, pulling off his rough woollen cap. He spoke in Welsh, but the attention of everyone was on the dark figure across the horse's back. Nimue saw, with nausea rising in her throat, that beneath the muck and mud, the man's doublet had been jewel-coloured, rich. She did not need the confirmation of the name that was being repeated, babbling mouth to mouth. It was Ralph Tollaster. And he was dead.

One of the maids, a hand at her mouth, was crying, noisy sobs, and Morfydd had a stout arm round her shoulders. Nimue saw that it was Eira, who had been sweet on the bailiff.

'Is he dead?' Gilbert asked in a voice that was strained high. His lips were tight and white, and as she looked at him, Nimue knew with intuitive certainty why he had returned alone that afternoon, why he had held himself in that fierce, white intensity. He had killed Ralph Tollaster.

And she knew too, why he had done it. It was for the gold. He had killed in a frenzy because the man had refused to part with that small, black rock, the rock which promised riches beyond price, which, veined with gold, was the key to untold secrets yet to be revealed.

Jonas Mowas's voice was no longer easy and wine-fuddled, he was asking questions, and the men were replying. They gestured back behind them, they were speaking of finding the body. But Nimue, sickened, could only look at Gilbert, and suddenly he caught her gaze and saw she knew the truth.

As violently as though she had challenged him, he moved, cutting across the confusion in the yard. He went to the pony and lifted the body, turning up the head by the hair. Then, with the dagger from his belt, he slit the sodden doublet and shirt, pulling them roughly aside while a scream of horror came from the women. He turned, breathing hard.

'See the terror in his eyes,' he shouted hoarsely. 'Yet there is not a mark on him. What else has caused this but sorcery?'

'Witchcraft,' hissed Dorabella, at his shoulder, in a voice that was thin and darting as the tongue of a snake. 'Witchcraft.' She held out a finger, straight at Nimue. 'There is a witch among us.'

Dorabella did not need to be told what Gilbert had done, she knew the worst of him, but he was hers now, and she was with him. United in defiance of the truth, they stood together and Nimue felt the sharp pricks of panic begin to touch her coldly, clammily, as she saw what was in their eyes, and how some of the servants were murmuring fearfully and crossing themselves, though Jonas Mowas had made a gesture of protest.

She tried to speak, calmly, rationally, before something born of ignorance and superstition spawned grotesquely among them is all its ugliness. But she knew her voice was unsteady, and her legs had begun to tremble beneath her.

'Whoever committed this terrible deed will surely, like the coward he is, try to shift the blame from his crime. I am no witch, there is no sorcery in this. The marks of violence may only be visible on a closer examination of the body, but even if there are none, there are many ways of provoking death.'

'You of course would know of such things,' Mary said deliberately. Her breast was heaving, and there was a strange

170

bright smile on her mouth. 'Was not your father the wizard skilled with poisons? And do you not grind strange herbs and powders in your chamber, secret from the concerns of the house? Oh, I have seen what you keep in that satchel, Madam Wizard's Daughter, the great crystal that summons demons, the charts with the signs of the Evil One upon them - .'

'In the name of heaven, Mary,' Nimue cried, feeling sheer horror laying a paralysing hold on her. But Mary turned to the others, her small features distorted like those of a wild cat, spitting.

'She consorts with Satan,' she cried, her breath coming in shallow gasps, and a moan went up from the assembled servants though again there was a protest from Jonas Mowas.

'A witch! A witch!' It was a low, rumbling murmur from someone, taken up by other voices.

Nimue tried to speak, but her throat was stiff.

'I am no witch. My father was an astrologer.'

'They are all of the same colour,' pronounced Dorabella inexorably, her pale eyes gleaming. 'What does holy church decree? Thou shalt not suffer a witch to live - . And she has killed Mister Tollaster - .'

'I have killed no-one, and you know it, Dorabella,' Nimue said clearly, her fear turning to incredulity and disgust. She rounded on the others, trying to make them see. 'This is the cant of superstition, ignorance and fear. You all know me, you know very well that I am not a witch, to work spells against others in the dark, to commit murder. You are distraught, Dorabella, and as for you, Mary, and your talk of consorting with Satan - .'

'Mister Tollaster had dealings with the devil,' Mary breathed, her nostrils flaring as she hissed the low words, and Nimue spun round. There was secretive knowledge in the other young woman's eyes, and the ring of truth in her voice. Having glimpsed the power of the dark, Mary had not been deterred by Nimue's refusal to aid her, but had unerringly sought out the one person in the household who had knowledge of such things. Ralph Tollaster had indeed mixed with others who dealt in the black arts, the information had hung round him like a dark cloud and Mary had fallen foul of him – or rather, Nimue thought, scorn filling her as she tried to keep her sense of proportion, she had sought him out deliberately. And now, her guilty awareness emblazoned across her face, she was trying to escape the consequences of her own dark deeds.

'He boasted of it openly,' Mary went on, and one or two heads nodded agreement as she too reached out an accusing finger. 'And Madam Gwynne, the daughter of a wizard, was his familiar.'

There was a sudden silence, like the hush before thunder. Nimue's heart began to pound in thick, slow beats that sent the blood rushing to her head so that she felt dazed and faint. The moment, like so many since she had come to this wild country, seemed to have been always known, to be charged with significance and a sense of destiny.

There was an interruption. From out of the night, the sound of hooves and the nervous snorts of a horse ridden too fast and inexpertly emerged into the group in the yard like a clumsy black phantom, and while the horse shuddered to a standstill, the rider, sobbing almost fell from the saddle.

It was a woman, scarcely more than a child, her long hair streaming.

'Oh, *Duw, Duw* - ,' she wailed, and stumbled towards the nearest man, her hands clinging. It was Jonas Mowas, and he held her up, calling for more lights, peering into her face. They could all see the blood.

'Is it more murder?' queried the quavering voice of the dowager, and Jonas spoke tersely in Welsh to the child, who replied in a streaming torrent, shaking within his arm. Out of the incoherent babble, Nimue heard one word that brought her out of her trance in shock.

'Pendragon - .'

Careless, she started forward, pushing the men aside, as they all crowded to hear the child's thin, high moaning.

'What is it?' she demanded, unaware that she was screaming the words aloud. 'What has happened to Pendragon?'

In the confusion no-one noticed her agitation, and Jonas Mowas looked up as Gilbert broke in on the child, loudly saying:

'God's teeth, what is the matter?'

'It is trouble at Caerwen.' Jonas Mowas was not blustering now, he was steady as a rock. 'A gathering – Llwyd and Meirion Ffeis, and more of those who have been put out of their lands, they are desperate. If Gwil the Stone will swing, he says, he cares nothing, his wife and new born baby died today, and they will have blood, they will not be stopped - . They are saying they will smoke him out - .'

'Who? Who?' Nimue managed, though she knew from the ice that was freezing her chest, her throat, so that she could not breathe, could not speak the words aloud. 'Who?'

'They will have the wizard that brings them ill, that shrivels their children and spells them - . They are going to burn Pendragon - .'

Without conscious thought Nimue had turned, her feet carrying her surely up the staircase to her chamber, the dark no barrier to her for it was lit by the terrible fires of urgency and need. Her hands reached steadily for her cloak, and snatched up her father's satchel – though she did not know why nor what good the crystal or her father's legacy to her might do if Pendragon was burning.

She was gone like a ghost and had reached the stables even while the men were milling about in the torchlight in the yard, getting under each other's feet, shouting questions and bawling answers. She led out Cariad, and without bothering to wait and saddle the pony she had fled, gone into the night riding bareback, trusting the spirits of the old wizard and of her father to guide her the long road to Pendragon tower. She called on them aloud as she rode, setting Cariad a furious pace that might have broken the pony's legs through the stones and tangles of tree roots that barred the trackless way across the mountain.

'Wait for me - wait for me,' she cried into the empty night sky. 'I am coming.'

There were dark horses with her, the steeds of death, ridden by riders whose hands were white bones on their bridles, and the wind howled in a terrible lament. Nimue clung to Cariad, bent low, seeing nothing, hearing nothing, aware only of her blood pulsing through her veins in an agony of anticipation of what she would find awaiting her at the end of her journey.

13

Fire. She was seeing it again, the flames leaping up into the dark night sky, the timbers exploding fiercely in white-hot charred ash, and she was hearing again the voice that wailed in the night wind. As she swayed, lost in the vision, she realised that it was her own voice, that she was crying the words aloud:

'My love, my love, my love.'

Sickened, with the sense of night terror all about her, Nimue knew now the secret of her visions. The past, yes, but also the present, the future that she had foreseen when she had first set eyes on Pendragon. She had known, even then, that this was what the end would be. Fire. And her thought was not now for herself, but for her husband.

Pendragon tower was burning, and figures ran in and out between the flames, shrieking. She thought with despairing anguish that she might as well have been looking at a vision of hell itself, with imps and demons black against the eternal fires. They were cheering hoarsely as it burned, yelling across to each other, eldritch screams that were inhuman, bestial, devoid of all feeling. And somewhere, lost in that inferno, was her darling, her sweet lord, her love and her life.

She slid from her pony, unaware of the trembling in every limb, and ran forward towards the flames, reaching out her hands before her to shield herself from the fierce heat, Everything was wavering, quivering, as though nothing was real except this maelstrom of flame and terror.

Then, though she did not hear the hoarse shouting behind her, there were hands reaching out that seized her, and she was held captive, screaming and struggling impotently. The voice of Owain ab Owain sounded in her ears like the trumpet of doom.

'You can do nothing. The fire has a hold. It must burn. The wind fans the flames.'

'My husband is there,' Nimue screamed. She had never thought she could sound like a London fishwife, but she heard herself gabbling, crying, cursing them even, as she kicked out to free herself. Owain was towering beside her, and the dark-skinned hands that held her were those of Huw, whose deceptively frail fingers were like iron bands around her arms, keeping her prisoner.

All the names she could remember from her father's wild store of spirits were let loose to come in power and strike them dead, all of them, friend and foe alike, so that she could go to him, die with him if she had to, in the flaming tower. She did not want to live if he could not be saved.

And yet somewhere deep within herself, she was aware that she had always known of this, that it was fire which had parted them in the distant past, and fire which must just as inevitably part them now. Turning away, gulping for breath in the searing heat which dried the tears that choked her even as they streaked down her cheeks, smudging the smoke and soot into her skin and her hair and her eyes, she found she had stopped struggling at last and was sobbing quietly in Huw's arms, which did not comfort or console, but simply held her, detached.

175

For a moment, she rebelled again in outrage that Huw's acceptance was beyond the pains and the passions of mortal existence, but the spasm passed and then Nimue was strangely glad that he made no attempt to soothe her. At this moment of crisis, she needed to draw upon her own strength, her own wisdom and the awareness of an inevitability that was fated, something that had been decreed and set down long since in the book of the Recording Angel.

They might be parted, she might never see him again in this life, but nothing could separate them, since they were one, two halves of the same whole. Resignation flooded over Nimue's soul, in spite of her bitterness. She was her father's daughter, she had been born a wise child, and she must accept what she knew within her heart, the truth that was greater than all her human loving. Her husband had left her once again, to tread the path that had been marked for him, and she would see him no more until she too had passed the boundary into that strange country which would yet welcome her as a wanderer returning home.

She turned away, her eyes gritty and unseeing, and Huw led her back to her pony and helped her to mount. Then she sat, her cloak pulled close about shoulders that were straight now, a back that was erect, holding up her head proudly, staring ahead into the night. Huw walked beside her, leading the beast away from the flames that devoured her home, her husband, the dream that, as Will might have phrased it with his playwright's poetry, had been too beautiful for this workaday world.

As they left the shrieks behind and the trees closed round them, with the last gleam of the flames on the waters of a little dark pool, ice-rimmed, sanity returned. Nimue took deep breaths, lifting her chin, feeling the comforting warmth of Cariad's back beneath her, the motion of the pony's movements. She could think again, though her thoughts were piteous, wrapping themselves round her tired and shocked mind like a dark cloak. But the dark itself held comfort, and she seemed to hear her father's voice, calm in the midst of the terror and despair.

'Whether you go to meet God or the devil, Nimue, hold up your head and look him in the eyes.'

Pendragon was gone, but she had not lost him. She would never lose him again. But oh, she told herself, hugging her pain fiercely to her heart, it would be a lonely road to walk without him.

The morning came at last, with a pale daffodil dawn and a streaming sky, weeping, Nimue thought dully, the tears she ached from but could no longer shed. Some of the Pendragon people had taken her in, a dark goodwife with a fierce old face and a cap of the most spotless white linen.

Nimue considered wearily how, but for this night's work, she might have come round the Pendragon lands with her husband, perhaps in the summer when the evenings were soft gold over the mountains in the west, and the same goodwife would have curtseyed and given her a cup of ale and a Welshcake, exchanging a remark with her silent, lowering husband and bringing forward a stool, the only moveable piece of furniture in the tiny cottage room, dusting it off for the new mistress to sit. But this morning, the good woman was clucking and plying Nimue with hot milk and soaked crust, all but feeding her like a child, stroking the wet hair back from her face and making haste to dry the sodden cloak and shoes and rub Nimue's feet with a towel from the press, wafer thin and old, that smelled of lavender.

Time passed, and she was content to let it. There was no more feeling or grief in her, only nothing. And it was in this situation, sitting with her skirts kilted up before the fire, that the newcomer found her when he came.

Huw, who had left her to the goodwife's ministrations, had vanished into the early morning dark, but now he returned and there was a tall, plainly but richly cloaked man with him. The

177

goodwife, with a look and a quiet word from the newcomer, disappeared from the room, and Huw indicated Nimue's forlorn, drooping figure beside the fire, then he stepped impassively back to take up his stance at the cottage door with his hands pushed into the sleeves of his long robe. His dark face gleamed like polished wood, but his eyes were alive and glistening with wisdom.

'Mistress Gwynne?' the voice was cultured, but overlaid with a London drawl. Nimue looked up dully.

'My obediences, lady. I carry a private letter for you,' the man said, and took a rolled parchment from his doublet. He handed it to Nimue, who took it and then, seeing the great waxen seal that dangled from it, suddenly felt her skin prickle and her senses sharpen. She examined the seal.

'The arms of England? Sir, who are you?'

'A courier, only. But sent in the greatest haste to seek you out to deliver this letter as you see, from one whose word is paramount. I am instructed to place it into your hands alone, and when you have read it, to impart further information, and then to escort you personally to London for an immediate audience with her Gracious Majesty, the Queen.'

Nimue looked from his tired, handsome features with their secrecy and stamp of official business, with which she was well acquainted, for many such men had come and gone in the little house near London Bridge, held quiet conversation with her father, and left with no explanation for herself. Feeling a sense of destiny, she broke the seal and unrolled the parchment.

By personal courier to Mistress Nimue Gwynne.

Your father served us well, and his daughter must now perform the same services for the state. There is no other person whose qualities and anticedents match the needs of the moment.

Return with the courier of this letter. Speak to no-one, waste no time. We summon you on our business to avert great wrong.

Nimue, dazed, felt herself colour as her eyes scanned the last sentence on the parchment, and the signature.

Certain as that the stars keep their courses, the daughter of my other Welsh wizard will not fail her country nor her Sovereign Lady

Elizabeth R

'What does this mean?' she breathed, lowering her voice though she and the courier were alone save for the still figure of Huw, his robes glimmering silently in the shadows beyond the firelight.

'I am instructed to tell you that Her Grace has not forgotten your father nor yourself, lady, but times must bow to expediency.'

Nimue thought rather wryly that if she had doubted, those words were unmistakably those of the Queen, who was inclined to twist everything she said so that she covered her tracks to anticipate all eventualities – her early life and the many times she had feared she had taken her last breath in the face of the block and the axe, had taught her that, Gereint Gwynne had said.

'But how can I serve the Queen?' she asked, too overwrought for niceties. 'I have no political power, no influence, and I - .' Her voice shook. 'I have this past night lost my husband and my home.'

The courier's face did not alter. Personal suffering was not his business.

'In private, I am instructed to tell you that Her Grace has the greatest opinion of you, your father's daughter. She has need of your integrity, your loyalty, and your inherited gifts, powers and skills with magic, also your youth and innocence, for there is a threat to her kingdom and her person and you alone can avert it. She waits for you at Greenwich even now, and I will conduct you to her. There is no time to lose, you must prepare yourself and accompany me as soon as I have obtained a mount for you.'

Nimue looked helplessly towards Huw, but he had disappeared from his post at the door. She felt as though a great weight was descending upon her, pulling her limbs down, a heaviness settling on her shoulders. She was sick and weak, and she could not, after this terrible night, heed her father's instruction to face whatever might confront her fearlessly, and look it in the face.

'I cannot - ,' she began weakly, moving her head from side to side, but there was a sound outside and then, moving with strange authority, Owain ab Owain entered with Huw behind him. With his blind eyes, he sought out Nimue and ignoring the courier, came unerringly to her, taking her hand and pulling her to her feet.

'You are needed and must go,' he told her, his voice deep with the soft lilting turns of phrase that would unerringly lift her heart now whenever she heard them. 'The Queen of England is old and tired. You are young and fresh, and you have powers beyond the temporal. More, you are a Pendragon.'

As she stared, bewildered, he said, low and intense:

'Pendragons have been servants of the great since the Merlin gave his counsel to Arthur, son of Uther Pendragon, sometimes counsellors, sometimes kings, it is all the same. Their lines of destiny are linked. When you took on the name of Pendragon you assumed also the mantle of your calling, daughter of a wizard and wife of another.' He took her by the shoulders, so that she could feel how his hands trembled with age and with something else. She felt it, the power passing into herself from him, and her heart stirred a little, but still her mind was mutinous.

'I – I cannot,' she said, turning away, for too much had happened this night, and he leaned closer.

'In the name of your husband - .'

'My husband, he is dead,' Nimue burst out, suddenly roused to anger. 'You know yourself that he perished in the flames.'

There was a pause, while the courier, impelled, remained silent. Then:

'Perhaps he will return,' Owain said enigmatically and she shrugged.

'I am familiar with the dead. But his spirit will not comfort me, though.'

'You speak from the depths of grief, for you have been sorely tried,' Owain told her, and there was understanding in his voice, but also impatience. 'Trust him. Trust me.'

He bade Nimue put on her still wet cloak and her wet shoes, and when she had done so led her outside, while the courier still waited impassively. The morning was fresh and wild, with pale yellow light touching the glimpses of life on the newly budding trees, and the sky catkin-coloured. She thought bleakly that she had never seen such a day of promise, on this day when all promises seemed to have been broken, but the old man was watching her, and there was something in his face that silenced the words she would have spoken.

'If your husband is dead,' he said solemnly, 'all the more need for you to go, and go quickly. Stoneyathe nor the enforcers of the law will not forget this night, deeds have been done and someone will have to pay. If you are found here alone, who knows, child, it will be you.'

Nimue's sluggish mind began to force itself to think. Dorabella and Mary were open in their enmity now, and when they discovered that she had been Pendragon's wife their heightened sense of vindictiveness would be far greater than her own ability, at present, to protect herself. For now that Pendragon had gone, she was alone. And Gilbert, most of all, had reason to want her out of the way. Apart from the fact that she would stand between him and his ambitions for the Pendragon land and the gold, she knew that he had murdered Ralph Tollaster.

As Owain watched her silently, her thoughts ran on so that she lifted a hand involuntarily to her throat. Although Jonas Mowas and the other gentry were no doubt concerned enough over all that had happened and would wish to see justice done, would they be able to prevent a knife in the dark or powerful, anonymous hands round her neck?

The image of the bailiff, who had been well aware of the risks he took, and who had lain dead across a horse's back, sprang unbidden to her mind. Gilbert had already killed once, and he would kill again to save himself.

Nimue shuddered. 'What must I do?' she said, and Owain reached out and covered her hands with his own.

'Go, child, as soon as you may. Do not look back. There is nothing here for you now. Go as your Queen bids, for there is work for you. For the sake of Pendragon and my old friend and your husband, I will remain here, and take care for your interests, but Pendragon tower has burned and lies in ruins. Huw shall attend you, he will be loyal to the death, and Math will be your squire.'

'My husband? Where is his body? I must see him for the last time,' Nimue whispered, but his hand tightened on hers.

'No, child, remember only the man you loved and married. Do not torment yourself. Leave him to me. I will do all that is fitting for him. He is in safe hands.'

She bowed her head in reluctant acceptance, and felt him press a blessing on her hair.

'Now go,' he said.

And so, by the time the sun set in red-yellow as bright as the gold which had seduced men from time out of mind to violence and greed, the gold which was Nimue's wedding gift but seemed to have conspired to rob her of all that she held even more precious, they were within sight of the towers of Flint on their way to London and Greenwich, where an impatient monarch waited. They were four, Nimue with Huw and Math riding together, and a little apart, the courier sitting his horse easily, familiar with long hours in the saddle.

Once again a Pendragon had been summoned. And the newest and youngest of them, wearing her grief like a dark glittering cloak, was already beginning to make her peace with the fates and discover strength within herself – for had not her husband been proud of her because of that core of strength, and would he not have been the first to bid her let go of the dream and, while cherishing his memory, accept what life had to offer her without him? They would meet again, had not their moons eclipsed on the south nodes?

By the time they crossed from the wild Welsh country into the Marches and English soil, Nimue had only one thought in her mind to uphold her. She was a Pendragon, and she had been summoned. She owed it to the name that had been bestowed on her in love and faith by her husband, not to fail, but to answer the call.

She seemed to feel her father's presence beside her, strong and reassuring. Behind her on the saddle, the leathern satchel he had given her, containing the great crystal and the other implements of his calling – and now, hers – was securely fastened. It was all she carried with her on that desperate ride, that and his image, and the image of Pendragon himself, astride his great white horse, the dark hair blowing back from his scarred face, vibrant against the night.

She felt as though they were riding with her, her father and her husband, bearing her company. And behind them, those other ghostly Pendragons who had been summoned and had answered the call in times of need.

Resolutely, with the night breeze stirring her hair gently as a caress, she turned her face once again towards the great city of London, to where her past had lain – and where her future waited.

Merry Meet
And Merry Part
And Merry Meet Again

The story continues in
PENDRAGON: THE HAND OF GLORY